# High Horse

A Salt Mine Novel

Joseph Browning    Suzi Yee

Text Copyright © 2021 by Joseph Browning and Suzi Yee

Published by Expeditious Retreat Press
Cover by J Caleb Design
Edited by Elizabeth VanZwoll

For information regarding Joseph Browning and Suzi Yee:

Subscribe to their mailing list at their website: https://www.joseph-browning.com

To follow them on Twitter: https://twitter.com/Joseph_Browning

To follow Joseph on Facebook: https://www.facebook.com/joseph.browning.52

To follow Suzi on Facebook: https://www.facebook.com/SuziYeeAuthor/

To follow them on MeWe: https://mewe.com/i/josephbrowning

## *By Joseph Browning and Suzi Yee*

### THE SALT MINE NOVELS

| | | |
|---|---|---|
| Money Hungry | Hen Pecked | Dark Matter |
| Feeding Frenzy | Brain Drain | Silent Night |
| Ground Rules | Bone Dry | Better Half |
| Mirror Mirror | Vicious Circle | Soul Mates |
| Bottom Line | High Horse | Swan Song |
| Whip Smart | Fair Game | Deep Sleep |
| Rest Assured | Double Dutch | |

# Chapter One

Bad Rothenbrunnen, Vorarlberg, Austria
30th of April, 10:00 p.m. (GMT+2)

The waxing moon cast a pale light over the stark white landscape, spectrally illuminating the rigid corners of a remote spa still covered with snow high in the Austrian Alps. Like the other lodges in the Grosses Walsertal Biosphere Reserve farther down the mountain, it was closed for the transition of seasons until the first alpine hikers arrived. It was the perfect time for a clandestine occasion.

To call it a sale or market would be vulgar. It was an off-books auction for people of means and discerning tastes. Most of the items were stolen or of too questionable provenance to be sold in legitimate auction houses. A few were even magical, and those attuned to the arcane were always among the buyers.

Alicia Elspeth Hovdenak Moncrief certainly had the connections to be invited to such an event, but that wasn't her style. She had no interest in funding such endeavors and the vultures that fed on the industry, but that didn't mean she was going to walk away from that which she sought.

She pulled her military-grade binoculars to her eyes and

the entrance of the exclusive spa retreat lit up in its night vision mode. The spa was privately owned and backed into the Europaschutzgebiet Gadental, a nature reserve that had not been commercially developed like the Great Walser Valley to the west.

Crouched beside Moncrief was Nalin Buchholz—codename Hobgoblin—who was looking through his own pair of binoculars. The two guards manning the front were armed with Steyr AUGs. Another guard made a circuit with a pair of Dobermans, and at last count, there were at least four other guards inside. They traded shifts every hour.

"Must be one hell of a mineral bath for that much security," he drily remarked.

"The waters are said to have healing properties," she murmured.

"They always say that," he sardonically replied. He checked his gut and for once, it was in complete agreement with his brain. "I don't like it."

"You don't have to," Moncrief reassured him as she got ready. "You just have to stay with the car and be my exit strategy. And if things go pear-shaped, my plan B."

Buchholz shook his head. He knew that voice. She had already made up her mind and his only decision was whether he was going to help her. He couldn't even evoke Leader; Moncrief was on her own time.

"Are you sure you don't want me to come with you?" he

offered.

She looked up and gave him a condescending smile made more palatable by the genuine glint of appreciation in her blue eyes. "That's sweet, but you'd just slow me down. Trust me. I've been doing this since I was eighteen and I haven't gotten caught yet."

Buchholz smirked. "What do you call Munich?"

"A misunderstanding that worked itself out," she euphemistically brushed aside the past near miss. It was simplicity itself. She should be in and out with the goods in no time, and she would be on the other side of the Atlantic before anyone knew something was missing.

"Can you hear me?" she whispered into the mouthpiece so softly it was barely audible to the naked ear.

"Crystal clear," she heard him through her own earpiece.

"Try not to blow anything up out of boredom," she teased him as she locked into her skis.

"Don't leave me out here for too long," he playfully cautioned her before seriously adding, "Be careful."

She nodded and lowered her goggles. He watched her take off into the night, following the countless tire tracks toward the resort nestled into the high peaks of the Central Alps before disappearing into cover. There had been a lot of traffic in the past forty-eight hours for a resort that was closed for the season, and the auction was due to take place tomorrow night.

The surface melt from the afternoon sun had refrozen,

sparing her from skiing in slush. She hit the ice with her poles and propelled herself across the packed snow. Born to a Norwegian mother, Moncrief was in skis not long after she could walk. She kept to the road for a while before veering off onto an animal trail. The nocturnal off-piste skiing added to the thrill of her endeavor. No one had groomed these trails; they were wild and untamed, and she made quick work of them.

Moncrief stayed downwind and circled wide to the back of the complex. She stashed her skis and poles behind a woodpile and found a concealed spot near the back entrance to the kitchen. From her large backpack, she pulled out a pinwheel and a baggie of bone-shaped biscuits—the first for the guard and the latter for the dogs. She threw a few biscuits in the snow, creating a trail that led to her hiding place.

Moncrief didn't cook much, but she had baked the batch of dog biscuits herself for the occasion. It was an old family recipe originally designed to calm restless hounds wound up after a vigorous hunt; everyone in the Moncrief household wanted a good night's sleep sans baying. In recent years, she'd repurposed them and updated the recipe—substituting bacon for suet in the savory treat—but the magic was the same: one nibble and they would be the most laid back Dobermans for the rest of the night.

Then, she waited, pinwheel in hand. As the guard turned the corner, the motion sensor light flooded the area. The dogs smelled the treats and deviated from their typical patrol path. The guard gave the line some slack and followed their lead; there was little point in having dogs if one didn't take advantage of their heightened senses. He reached for his weapon when he finally saw Moncrief, but before he could unholster it, the harsh angles of his mercenary face softened in child-like wonder at the sight of the pinwheel's swirling colors, spinning faster with each visible puff of her breath.

He immediately dropped the leashes when she reached out to hand it to him. He was utterly captivated by it and knocked it with his finger when it started to slow. He'd be occupied until someone took it away from him—the pinwheel was an early twentieth century must-have for practitioners of the arts with fussy children in the age before TV or electronic devices. The keyring at his side jingled as he sat down in the snow and she could have easily taken it off him, but finding the right key was always a hassle and she'd come prepared.

"*Bleib*," she said to the compliant dogs and they immediately obeyed. She patted them on their heads and dropped another handful of biscuits at their feet as she hustled toward the building. The clock had officially started. The patrol took a little less than an hour to complete a circuit, so the guards in the front wouldn't miss him or the dogs for another forty-five minutes.

When she got to the kitchen door, she pulled out her skeleton key, a shortened and sculpted human femur that had been enchanted to fit any keyhole. It worked wonderfully on conventional locks, but was no help with magnetic or RFID locks as it had been made over two hundred years ago when the latest tech trend was installing gas lamps in the home. Fortunately, the back door to the kitchen was not deemed a high security risk and had a standard lock.

She slid the shaved graduated slope of the bone into the hole and spoke the activation words. The bone vibrated and expanded, filling in the empty space to perfectly fit against the pins and tumblers. When she felt it still in her hand, she turned the key and entered.

The kitchen was packed away for the season, and she quietly crept from one draped station to another until she found the door to the cellar. She shimmed her way through the racks of wine to a door along the back wall. She'd spent enough time with Wilson to recognize the nigh-unpickable Bowley lock on it.

She knew she had the right door based on its top-end lock, but she wasn't going to be able to unlock it with the skeleton key. It worked against old-style warded locks but not the modern Bowley wards. Additionally, she didn't have the very specific lockpick tools needed to open it on the fly.

She summoned her will to scan the door for magical protections, in particular checking for things prohibiting human passage. She smiled mischievously when she found none and extracted the unwieldy miner's pick from her backpack. It dated back to the California gold rush and her family had acquired it at the turn of the last century after foiling a robbery against one of their Glaswegian banks. Made by a practitioner who feared cave-ins, it created a short-lived extra dimensional bubble that allowed the holder to pass through any solid material except salt. She funneled a little of her will into the tool and stepped through the thick steel door unscathed and undetected.

Inside, the two security cameras were as her source described: covering most of the room but not all of it. *This would have never happened on Wilson's watch*, she mentally chided them as she set up shop in the small blind spot. Thing went much faster with both hands free, and she pulled out a matchbox and a doll's blanket: a quilted patch six inches square with roses on one side and daisies on the other.

With daisy side up, she emptied the matchbox of its contents—a varied collection of miniature tools—in its center and folded in the corners. She quietly spoke the incantation.

If wishes were horses, beggars would ride.
If turnips were watches, I'd wear one by my side.
If "ifs" and "ands" were pots and pans,
There'd be no work for tinkers' hands.

The square enlarged twelve times and everything came up roses. The tools were now full-sized, lying on the blanket that measured six feet by six feet. She wasn't sure if she'd need any of them, but loathed needing a hex screwdriver and not having one. She hurriedly pushed the tools to the side before brandishing Carnwennan and fading from sight.

She moved through the room of artifacts, grabbing anything she recognized as old Yiddish books or unrecovered Nazi plunder and placing them on the blanket. There was nothing she could do about the books that were already burned or the precious objects that had been melted into bullion, but she—like her parents and her grandparents before her—was doing her part. None of these things were magical, but they were priceless to the people from whom they'd been taken.

Once she got everything she recognized, she carefully arranged the paintings, statues, books, and small household items on the center of the blanket, making adjustments to get as much as she could in this run. When the pile reached a precarious mass with the addition of her tools, she folded up the corners until there were only daisies showing and softly sang the incantation.

Lucy Locket lost her pocket,
Kitty Fisher found it;
Nothing in it, nothing in it,
But the lace 'round it.

The blanket shrank back down to six inches and with it, all its contents. She packed everything folded inside the blanket into the matchbox and used cotton fluff to cushion them from damage. Then, she wrapped the matchbox in a handkerchief and placed it in a small waterproof scuba bag. The little doll's blanket was returned to its usual compartment in her backpack.

Moncrief checked her watch to make sure she was on time and gave herself five minutes to browse with a bit of magical assistance. She palmed a small rock—the perfect size for throwing or skipping over the water—and ran her fingers over its familiar contours.

When famed Maryland witch Moll Dyer was accused of witchcraft in the seventeenth century, she was driven out of town by her neighbors and died of exposure on a boulder. Moncrief wasn't sure how a piece of that boulder came into her family's possession, but she never went on a retrieval or shopping trip without it. Like a dousing rod to water, this stone led the way to magical items.

There were always small pieces of practical magic to be had: needles that never broke, jewelry that enhanced appearance or smoothed out an unfortunate voice, pens that never ran out of ink, etc. The world had moved on from magical solutions to everyday problems and many had been discarded unwittingly by non-practitioners over time. However, enchanted items that were fine or valuable in their own right were more likely to survive, and the young heiress had snatched up many a find at regular auctions and antique shops when she held the stone in hand.

As she walked the aisles with Arthur's dagger in one hand and the stone in the other, she felt something tug on her will and she followed it, stopping before a handsome gold pocket watch on a chain. Without doing more investigation, she had no way of knowing what the watch did, magically speaking. She did a quick scan to check for curses and tucked it into her pocket when she found none.

As she turned another corner, she was taken aback by a strong jerk from the stone. It was usually more subtle in its guidance, which meant something potent was lurking nearby. That piqued her interest. *What kind of high magic is up for auction here?* she thought, cautiously approaching a sealed case and noting the enhanced security upon it with a thread of her will.

Within were eight yellow candles held in a plain silver menorah. Based on their intact wicks, they had never been lit and she could feel their vile aura when she put her face near the glass. A sense of dread came over her as she read the crimson sigils etched down their sides. They were anguish candles.

*Shit.* Moncrief had packed heavy, but not eight anguish candle heavy. She checked the time—whatever she was going to do, she had to do it fast.

She returned to the cameras' blindspot and put her full-sized magical loot away in her backpack. The doll's blanket was strictly for mundane things because it was ill advised to place enchanted items into esoterically folded extradimensional spaces.

"We've got a problem," she whispered.

Buchholz sat up as Moncrief's voice came in through his earpiece. "Are you okay?"

"Yeah, but I may kick a hornet's nest on the way out," she murmured. He could hear the wince in her words.

"It better be worth it," he warned her.

"They're selling anguish candles," she said simply. "Eight of them."

Buchholz felt like he'd been kicked in the gut. His whole life had been spent in the shadow of what his nation and fellow countrymen had perpetrated in the name of nationalism and eugenics, and it didn't get prettier when he'd found out about the magical aspects of the Holocaust. "Can you safely extract them?"

"I think so," she verified. "But I may need you to deploy plan B."

Buchholz was already unpacking weapons from his trunk. "Coming in loud and clear."

Moncrief pulled out a pair of finely linked chain gloves— hermetically grounded to withstand the worst magical mojo— and the small containment box she always carried on her retrieval missions because she never knew when she was going to run across something interesting or dangerous. Once she had the gloves on, she got the miner's pick back out and looked at the case one more time. She had a good feeling about her idea, but she activated Hermes's wings on her boots just in case she set off an alarm and had to make a hasty retreat.

Using the pick's magic, she plucked three candles out and they disappeared from sight as she closed her hand around them. Even through the gauntlets, she could feel them pulse and writhe. She funneled a little more of her will into the pick and ushered them through the glass, breathing a sigh of relief once the candles passed without issue. It wasn't easy juggling Carnwennan, the pick, *and* the candles, but she'd done it.

She deposited the first batch in the box and went in for another, buoyed by her ingenuity and initial success. She had just pulled the last two candles from the menorah when she heard footsteps and voices from the other side of the door.

Scurrying, she closed the containment box and sealed it with her will—effectively isolating it from scrying or magical tracking—and then chucked everything in her backpack. She knew the cameras never had eyes on her so she should be safe to walk out once the door opened, invisible due to Carnwennan's magic.

Suddenly her good feeling drained away—the dagger didn't provide invisibility in the infrared spectrum, and anyone with night vision gear would see her as plain as day. She pressed herself against the wall and drew deep from the well of her will, opting for a quick escape instead of a sneaky one. Sometimes, karma struck in unexpected ways.

She checked her watch and the seconds ticked by as she

waited. The pent-up magic coursed through her veins like a coiled spring waiting to be released. As soon as the thick iron door opened, she raced out, bolstered by Hermes's wings. Even though she was five feet two and a 122 pounds, the sheer velocity of her escape bowled the two armed guards onto their backs. She retraced her steps and found the guard and the dogs where she had left them thirty-nine minutes ago.

She unholstered the guard's Glock and tossed it far away into a snowbank as he blissfully spun the pinwheel. She retrieved her skis, snapped into them, and skied back to the guard. Readying herself for a quick getaway, she plucked the pinwheel out of his hands then took off like a shot. As soon as she was out of his line-of-sight, she tucked the child's toy into one of her jacket pockets and rushed back toward the car.

The guard moaned groggily as he came to—why was he sitting on the ground and why were the dogs looking at him with big goofy eyes? It took him a second to register that he no longer had his gun before he remembered seeing a woman throwing it into the snow moments before. He didn't know why he'd let her do that in the first place. He shouted out as he took to his feet and grabbed the dogs' leashes. He tried to run toward the snowbank to retrieve his weapon, but the Dobermans refused to budge. The biscuit lady had told them to stay and that's exactly what they were going to do, at least for the next fifteen minutes or so.

Moncrief heard his cries over the sound of snow under

her skis and picked up speed, making a beeline to Buchholz. She flinched at the sound of the first shot and started evasive maneuvers. "Any time, Hobgoblin!" she called out over the comm.

"Just waiting for the word," he replied and added, "Don't look back."

Moncrief was too busy trying to keep as many trees as possible between her and the firing guards to see the missile arch overhead, but she heard the impact and explosion. Nothing says "don't pursue" like a rocket launcher and Buchholz always seemed to have one on hand, no matter where he was or how short of notice. Were it earlier in the season, she would have been concerned about starting an avalanche, but there hadn't been any heavy snow in over a month and it was almost May.

She eased off the magic in her boots as soon as she saw the car. Buchholz had already put away his toys and started the engine. She gently came to the stop within feet of the back and popped her winter sports gear into the car.

"Enjoy your ski?" he humorously inquired as she entered the toasty vehicle.

"It was invigorating," she replied with a smile. "But I've got a plane to catch."

# Chapter Two

The Salt Mine never slept, but it was run by people and people needed sleep. Every agent eventually had cause to hit the Mine afterhours: usually a pick up or drop off. Superficially, it looked the same—a guard at the guard station, a polite yet firm gatekeeper on the first floor, and analysts plugging away at too many screens deeper within—but there was something undeniably odd about the Salt Mine at night. It was a whole other beast when it was staffed by the graveyard shift.

Theo Kleeson had his doubts when he applied for the night guard position, but it ended up being the best job he'd had in a long time. Once the second shift handed off to the third, he had hours to himself. Sure, it put a damper on his social life, but so did being broke.

Tonight, he was puffing away on a cigar inside the guard station, something he wasn't allowed to do at home and wasn't technically supposed to do here because there were explosives stored somewhere on site. He figured it was fine because this station was for passenger traffic onto Zug Island, and even if he was working the entrance that took freight, no one delivered combustibles in the dead of night—score another point for night shift.

He saw the headlights of the black Range Rover long before it got to the gate, giving him plenty of time to put out the cigar and give the small hut a good airing out. Kleeson recognized the SUV and he'd be damned if he got fired over something as trivial as smoking on the job.

It came to a stop and the tinted windows rolled down. Its driver presented his ID: David LaSalle, Executive Assistant at Discretion Minerals.

"Forget something at the office, Mr. LaSalle?" Kleeson joked before handing him back the card and pressing the button inside the guard station to raise the gate.

"Something like that," the crisp tenor replied before applying a dash of magic in his words. "But you didn't see me here and you aren't going to remember the next car you let through after me either."

The guard smiled and winked. "You know me. Keep my head down and my mouth shut."

"Good man," LaSalle replied as he pulled his ID and his will back into the vehicle. He steered the SUV toward Discretion Minerals' underground parking garage and parked in one of the executive spaces. There were no names or assigned numbers printed on the concrete, but everyone who worked there knew to park somewhere else.

Although it was the middle of the night, LaSalle had felt compelled to put on a suit before coming back to the office. It wasn't a requirement, but it felt wrong to come in wearing pajamas or casual wear. What lay ahead of him was serious business and a man should always dress for the task at hand.

LaSalle entered the elevators and engaged his titanium key, causing the lift to go down to the first floor of the Salt Mine. When the doors opened, the buxom Angela Abrams was no longer manning the entry. Night shift had taken over.

"Good evening, Mr. LaSalle," Cheryl Holiday greeted him from behind the ballistic glass. It was a dead heat on which was thicker: her sable locks or her lush voice. Even the tinny speakers could not diminish the luster of its resonance. "Are we expecting a visitor this evening?"

The metal slot opened up and he placed his possessions inside. "More like an unexpected delivery, Ms. Holiday," he corrected her.

She discreetly ran her eyes over his form while the machine whirled—he was always the nicest looking thing she'd see during any of her shifts.

"Who will be the delivery man?" she asked as lines of data streamed across her screen.

"Delivery woman," he corrected her. "Ms. Moncrief should be arriving within the next hour."

Holiday had worked here long enough to ask no more questions, but she pulled out the personal protective equipment all the same. She shouldn't have any direct contact with whatever was coming in, but the more layers between it and her, the better.

Once everything passed security, she opened the door into the Salt Mine and his items moved to the other side of the threshold. He strode with purpose across the entryway and Holiday lapped up the view.

"I'll be setting up. Let me know when the package arrives," LaSalle said politely, ignoring her leering.

"Understood, Mr. LaSalle," she confirmed the request. When he was out of view, Holiday donned her gloves and protective eye wear before restarting her audio book, but left the lead apron slung on the wall. It was so heavy and she should have plenty of time to put it on while the package rode down to the first floor.

LaSalle's steps echoed on his way to the next set of elevators, but he was not going lower into the Mine. Instead of summoning one of the lifts, he held his titanium key against a hidden panel on the wall. Only a few keys opened the door to the secreted section, and his was one of them.

He entered the narrow hallway and the door closed behind him. At six feet three and 230 pounds, he barely fit in the passage. He had to bend at the knees when he went through and there was only a scant two inches of clearance on either side. He was glad he wasn't claustrophobic.

The area was carved out of the salt, but the floor, walls, and ceiling were all covered in titanium. Titanium was inert in every sense, including magically, and pure titanium was completely rust and corrosive resistant. In these passages and rooms, they couldn't afford any weak spots for unwanted magic to leech in or escape. Etched into the titanium were glowing blue sigils—a magical gauntlet of sorts. It kept out supernatural creatures and suppressed malevolent magic, but it was impossible to ward against everything.

That's where LaSalle came it. It was his job to make sure none of the agents were compromised after encountering supernatural creatures, magical items, and practitioners in general. If they brought in questionable items, this was where they were assessed before further entry into the Salt Mine— like customs, but with less paperwork and more quarantine. While agents were given plenty of esoteric inoculation and protective gear, LaSalle was the last line of defense and he took the responsibility seriously. Every encounter had the possibility of being his last if he didn't.

At the junction, he took a left and opened the second door. The room was all sharp lines meeting in unharmonious angles. It was like walking into one of Picasso's later works—no matter how long you looked, you couldn't decide if that was an eye or a nose.

The architecture of a space and the things within it could block or promote the flow of energy—similar to feng shui without the Eastern connotation—and this room was deliberately fashioned to disrupt and trap magical energy. He'd arranged the furniture to accommodate a single agent in a way that promoted those efforts. It was just another factor to tip the scales in his favor; he wasn't taking any chances with anguish candles.

When everything was set up, LaSalle stepped back into the hallway. The room was ideal for bringing in high-level artifacts of known malevolent energy, but it was highly unpleasant to wait inside. In spite of the physically cramped conditions in the hall, it was preferable to the metaphysical constraints of the room. He popped in his earbuds and closed his eyes as John Coltrane's "A Love Supreme" started. The music took him somewhere else, and he centered himself for what was to come.

Holiday's voice cut through the saxophone. "Ms. Moncrief just entered the elevators." LaSalle paused his music and walked down the magically warded passage back into the foyer. He summoned his will and began his observation immediately.

Moncrief wasn't wearing the performative facade of Alicia, jaunty heiress to the Hovdenak shipping and Moncrief real estate fortunes. There was no impeccable polish to her hair and makeup, or designer outfits with matching accessories. Dressed in jeans and a sweater with her blonde hair in a ponytail, even Clover looked different during the night shift, although he expected that her jeans still cost more than his entire suit.

As she chatted with Holiday, he could see her face was animated with its normal spontaneous expressions, but her eyes were tired. He could imagine how exhausting it was to spend that much time with eight anguish candles, even if they were in a containment box. Tonight, she was just another agent who'd had a long day.

Holiday smiled brightly, but her eyes never left the screen. Whatever was in that box was contained, but just barely. She was glad she had donned her protective gear. Without missing a beat in the conversation, Holiday pressed a series of buttons that lit up a sequence of lights on LaSalle's side of the entrance—both Moncrief and the package had passed security in their current state.

A number pad appeared on the wall and he punched in a code, giving Holiday permission to let both pass into the Salt Mine. The attendant diverted the box to LaSalle and pressed the button that opened the door for Moncrief to pass.

"Everything looks fine," she said to Moncrief as the door opened. "Have a good evening, Ms. Moncrief."

"And you are well, Cheryl," Moncrief reflexively responded. "Ah, David. So good to see you," she said after passing over the threshold. "I see you have my package."

He motioned her into the hallway—he didn't like to chat before the process. If an agent was affected, it would only distract him.

"Right, I know the drill," she self-corrected and silently entered the gauntlet. She had been through the process a number of times—coming in contact with dangerous magical objects happened with some regularity.

She wasn't a traditional Salt Mine agent. She had no aliases, as Alicia Moncrief was the keystone onto which other agents hung theirs. Her vast resources, extensive business and philanthropic operations, and membership among the old magical families made her an unlikely recruit for a governmental agency, but Leader had persisted.

Eventually, they came to a mutually beneficial arrangement. Moncrief remained the high-spirited socialite publicly but became Clover in the shadows. Having a codename made her feel like an arcane female Batman, only less broody and better dressed. But she still had her own thing that predated the Salt Mine, a sense of mission she refused to relinquish. Thus, it wasn't uncommon for her to bring in something captured on her own initiative.

The Salt Mine had the luxury of space and a vetted staff to deal with nasty magical items that were beyond what she could handle on her own in the Moncrief family vault. Her preference was generally destruction or neutralization of bad magic, but if that could not be safely done, she entrusted it to the Mine. In exchange, the Mine had unprecedented access to a whole other echelon of generational knowledge and wealth.

Moncrief was intimately familiar with almost all the sigils and runes that glimmered in the titanium all around her—her parents had groomed her to be more than a wife and mother of capable practitioners. She stepped into the open door and sat down in the only seat.

She prepared herself for scanning. It went easier for both of them if she didn't resist. When she'd started working with the Salt Mine, the process stuck in her craw, not because it was invasive but because it was insulting that someone would think a Moncrief could be so easily swayed or manipulated. She was young and still heavily dosed on the idea of breeding, but she had since been disabused of the notion. Evil was real and indifferent to her pedigree.

Eventually she started viewing it as a relief, like getting checked out by a healthcare provider. If LaSalle said she was good, she was good. Admittedly, since starting the scanning process she may have pushed for more dangerous game knowing she'd have a chance to get cleaned up later, but that was a different issue altogether.

LaSalle closed the door behind him and started the scan. Moncrief froze in place as he slowly peeled back her layers. Superficial changes could be given a pass as long as the deeper levels were still sound, especially if they were consistent with long-term trends and the agent's basic personality. It was the metaphysical equivalent of trying a new hair cut, changing up an exercise routine, or sliding back into bad habits—agents could try on different hats as long as it was being put on the same head.

He breathed a sigh of relief when he found of the cut of her jib unchanged. Then, he took a razor of his will and sliced open the containment box. The energy from the candles flew out, rebelling against confinement. LaSalle stood guard over himself and Moncrief while it flew in all directions. The room acted like an anechoic chamber, absorbing and decelerating magical energy until the candles unloaded the excess energy they'd generated while in the containment box. After they wore themselves out, he laid them out on the table with his gloved hand for initial inspection: eight anguish candles.

Binding ghosts into enchanted items as a power source was an old practice among magicians, but Nazi practitioner Albrecht Spitzer had taken it one step further. Using the prisoners held in Chelmno, he invented a way to ritually sacrifice people and trap their souls for later use by making tallow candles from the fat rendered from their bodies—effectively creating occult batteries preloaded with horrific numbers of ghosts. The sigils were carved with the bones of the dead and colored in with ink made from their blood mixed with their burned ashes. Thousands died in the camp before Spitzer had perfected the ritual, and only one batch was made, producing 777 anguish candles.

Much of the practice of necromancy was banned after World War II, and on paper, all of the anguish candles were accounted for. Many of them were destroyed in the nuclear tests of the 1950s and 60s, although the Salt Mine harbored suspicions that the Ivory Tower had fudged their numbers.

LaSalle nestled the candles in a dish of salt, making sure

they were complete covered. They were going to spend a week in isolation before anyone would be allowed to examine them. There was enough negative energy implicit in anguish candles without residual rub off from being stored with other Nazi plunder.

He withdrew his will and watched her eyes to make sure she returned unscathed. Moncrief blinked a few times and breathed on her own volition. He handed her a bottle of water and pronounced, "You're good."

She took a large drink and smiled wide. "Music to my ears."

"Did Hobgoblin spend any time with the uncontained candles?" LaSalle asked for completeness.

"No, just in the car ride to the airport, but they were already in the box by then," she answered.

"He didn't fly back with you?" he inquired to get a true estimation of potential exposure.

She shook her head. "No, he had other engagements."

LaSalle made a note in his tablet for the next time Hobgoblin came in for a tune-up.

# Chapter Three

Mount Vernon Place, Maryland, USA
1st of May, 2:30 p.m. (GMT-4)

A firm knock landed on the double doors of the dim fourth-floor suite. "Miss, it's half past two," the sonorous baritone informed her from the landing.

Moncrief pulled back the lower edge of her silk sleep mask to verify the time and flinched at the bright light that seeped in along the seam of the curtains. "Thank you, Gerard," she replied loudly. "I'll be out in a few."

"I brought coffee and croissants," he said neutrally. "Shall I send it back to the kitchen?"

"No," she quickly objected and rolled around in bed, trying to find her robe. She made quite a ruckus in the clumsy state of half-wakefulness. "Please bring them in."

The uniformed butler waited an appropriate amount of time before opening the door. He found his mistress disheveled but decent. "Good afternoon, miss," he greeted her and placed the tray on the bed beside her. She immediate went for the carafe of coffee while he drew back the heavy curtain but left the sheer privacy one in place. "Did miss have a good trip?"

"Quite," she answered after a long drink. "But I'm due for the Derby. Aunt Bethany will already be cross with me for missing the Oaks today."

"Will miss no longer need her pink attire?" he inquired.

Moncrief gave it some thought. "I'll arrive in the pink silk Versace, but be sure to pack the sleeveless lavender Jacquard that I selected last week. And the hat and clutch I bought to go with it. Plus five days' clothing of the usual mix, just in case," she instructed him piecemeal as things came to mind. It had been a while since she made a visit to Kentucky, and one could never be sure how long these things would last.

He gave her a curt nod. "Very well, miss. And what time should I have the plane ready?"

She mulled this over a bite of croissant. She didn't want to arrive too late but she had work to do in the vault before she left. "Five hours should be enough time."

"I'll make the arrangements right away," he assured her on his way out. Gerard had become accustomed to her flights of fancy and late-night travel over the years. As long as she got home in one piece and remembered to eat something, he considered it a rousing success.

She enjoyed the rest of her breakfast in bed scrolling over pictures from Churchill Downs. The Kentucky Derby was always run on the first Saturday in May, but it was preceded by days of racing beforehand, not to mention a two-week long festival in the city. Traditionally, the day before the Derby was the Kentucky Oaks, dedicated to the ladies both equine and human, and everyone in attendance wore pink.

Moncrief had a passable knowledge about the sport of kings, but she was never really a horse person, even as a little girl. She rode competently and knew what qualities to look for in a mount, but she never got into tracing bloodlines, breeding, and handicapping. She'd known of too many families brought low by losses at the track and never put more at stake than she could stand to lose. It freed her to place bets on whimsy, choosing a horse whose name or appearance struck her fancy.

After she was dressed, she exited her suite and descended the wide wooden stairs that circled the walls of the expansive three-story foyer. In the heart of historic Baltimore, the Moncrief family home was a veritable mansion, but to her, it was simply home. She went to the back of the house and passed through the servants' domain before taking another set of stairs into the basement.

Past the larder, dry goods, supply room, wine cellar entrance, and the furniture that was too good to get rid of but no longer in use was an old iron door inlaid with silver and gold sigils. In addition to the static protections, living runes flashed in an ever-changing pattern, making this one of the most magically secure areas in the world; the only areas more secure were protected by governmental agencies like the Salt Mine and the Ivory Tower.

The spirits writhed at her approach. The first line of

protection was to subconsciously shoo away anyone that wandered this way. Moncrief was well accustomed to the aura, but when she was a small child it had sent her fleeing.

There were no keyholes or handles, only a Javanese kris hanging to the side. Moncrief picked up the asymmetrical dagger with the wavy blade and pricked her finger on its sharp tip. She had done it so many times, she knew just how much pressure to apply to the digit to form a full drop and no more.

She traced a pattern upon the smooth surface of the cold iron and the crimson smear vanished as the door absorbed her blood. There was no trace left on either her finger or the iron as the lock clicked open. She passed into the chamber beyond, closing the warded door behind her. While her dutiful staff readied for her next stint of travel upstairs, she took care of her work downstairs.

She'd stashed everything in the vault before crashing in her bed and found everything as she'd left it in the wee hours of the morning. Nothing had been put away, but at least it was secure while she caught some shut eye. She'd napped on the plane ride over the Atlantic, but her dreams were not pleasant with the anguish candles onboard. They had been small icy slivers of the past and they'd left her nearly as tired as she'd been prior to sleeping.

Moncrief methodically emptied her backpack, double-checking all the pockets and compartments. She returned all the miniature items back to full size and put away the doll's blanket along with all the other items she'd taken with her to Austria. After the theft and subsequent retrieval of Mictēcacihuātl's Tongue, she had gotten better about keeping track of inventory and putting things away between outings.

Now that she had the luxury of time, she paused to admire works of art that had not seen the light of day in decades—the large Picasso watercolor *Naked Woman on the Beach*, painted in Provence in 1923, the *Portrait of Mlle. Gabrielle Diot* by Degas, and Pissarro's charming *Rue de Village* to name a few. There were various Grecian inspired bronze statuettes, although the one depicting the muses was her favorite of the bunch. Being an only child, the idea of siblings held great charm.

Up to twenty percent of the art in Europe was looted by the Nazis starting as early as 1933. Despite the effort of the Monuments Men immediately after the war and the organizations that had come since, an estimated 100,000 items still had not been returned to their rightful owners. While some were sitting in plain sight in museums, others were hidden away in private collections. It was hard to identify everyday objects like stolen china, crystal, or silver, but the International Foundation for Art Research (IFAR) kept a list of the plundered art.

She set the pieces aside to be sent anonymously to IFAR. Many of them came with rewards, but she never accepted any. Seeing the piece listed as "recovered" the next time she hit the website was enough. The few old books that had been survived the German bonfires would go to YIVO Institute for Jewish Research, home to one of the world's foremost collections of Yiddish books and artifacts. If there was a way to hunt down their provenance, they would be able to do it. If not, at least they would be preserved and made digitally available to the public.

Mundane matters aside, she turned to the pocket watch. Being a timepiece, her first concern was temporal magic, one of the seven forbidden arts. There was a certain type of practitioner that was drawn to the taboo, even if it did threaten the integrity of reality. If it was altering time esoterically, she was going to have to destroy it.

There were various ways to identify the arcane properties of enchanted items. Some practitioners were able to cast spells or conduct rituals to know such things, while others would summon a creature and get them to identify it for them. For those with the time, materials, and inclination, they could approach it more scientifically, performing a series of tests in isolation to tease out its properties. For legendary or well-known objects, she could hit the stacks of either her own family library or the Salt Mine's.

Moncrief rarely used any of those options as she was fortunate enough to inherit her great-grandfather's arcane phoropter. The mundane version was a tool used by optometrists to check a person's vision; anyone who wore prescription corrective lens was well versed with the series of diagnostic flips to see which looked clearer: one or two. The same principles applied to this device, except the practitioner looking through the eye holes was looking for magical clarity, sharpened by trying a series of lenses enchanted to catch different magical spectrums.

She pulled out a well-worn journal from one of the bookshelves—a user's manual of sorts—and turned on the desk lamp for more light. Then, she placed the pocket watch on the table and put her face against the phoropter. Reaching up, her hands felt for the familiar knobs and levers on either side, making adjustments before everything came into focus.

The watch wasn't magical, but the chain was. She pulled back and translated the readings on the different dials. It was charmed with extra strength, persistent polish, and with a deterrent against pickpockets—quaint, but hardly useful these days. She examined the watch itself more closely and found a maker's mark and engraved initials. Given its proximity to other Nazi plunder, she would research it further, but first she had to deal with the chain.

It was the type of lesser item she routinely drained of esoteric power and siphoned into the family vault. The Moncriefs had long moved away from the barbaric practice of using ghosts, and instead supplemented their esoteric energy requirements with the glut of practical magic that had become passé.

Her parents had set up the system to gently strip an item of its magic without destroying it in the process. In fact, one of her favorite pair of earrings was once enchanted to hide smallpox scars. They had no arcane properties now, but that didn't make the rubies and diamonds sparkle any less.

She unhooked the chain from the pocket watch and walked it to the sandbox. Only in the Moncrief household did a child's sandbox hold pharaonic sand from the Valley of the Kings. She buried the chain in the sand and let it sit while she picked out items to take with her to Kentucky: an unbreakable needle and endless thread that color matched, a steadfast hat pin that would hold her fascinator in place once positioned, and a broach that allowed her to drink without getting drunk; they were serious about their bourbon in Kentucky and she wasn't as young as she used to be. She then set her sights on researching the watch.

After the chain had been sitting in the sand for an hour, she extracted it using the archeology sifter hanging on the wall beside the box. She reattached it to the pocket watch, which she had traced to a continental watchmaker using Swiss movement, produced some time after 1853 but before 1880. Many years of searching had honed her provenance-hunting skills. She usually knew when and where something had been made before the sand had done its work.

She scooped up the now-magically infused pharaonic sand with a bronze Roman batillum. The rectangular incense ash scooper wasn't magical, but it was just the right size and shape to deposit the sand into an Old Kingdom canopic jar. The pottery didn't have a colorful paint job or a decorative head as a top, but the side bore the cartouche of Heka, Egyptian god of magic and medicine. The unadorned alabaster jar slowly turned crimson as she filled it.

Once it was full, she secured the lid and left it to cook. Her Egyptophilic maternal grandparents had gifted the piece to her mother, who in turn attuned it to the vault. It transferred all the magic absorbed in the sand into powering the vault, and once the jar turned white again, the sand was ready to be reused.

She put everything away and turned off the lights before exiting the vault, sealing the family's magical treasures behind the iron slab. She would have liked to do more, but it could wait until she returned. She had to shower and dress for a party tonight, and tomorrow, spend a day at the races. The work of a socialite-slash-covert-operative was never done.

# Chapter Four

Matumaini Village, Ngara District, Kagera, Tanzania
1st of May, 10:45 p.m. (GMT+3)

The lone figure perched in the fields tightened the wrap around him as the chill of night crept in with the fog. The mist was insidious, slowing rolling in from the coast and blanketing the highland plateaus west of Lake Victoria. The moon was on the rise, making it marginally easier to see forms through the haze but not in any detail.

It was the middle of the spring rains, an important but vulnerable time for crops in the field. His village was situated between two game reserves connected by natural vegetation, making it a crucial corridor for animals to travel between the two. Herds of ungulates were known to pass through and feed on the hoof. Whatever wasn't eaten could easily be trampled underfoot by elephants, abruptly ending any hope of harvest. Packs of wild dogs thought nothing of snatching the chickens, and the rare larger carnivore saw their goats or cows as potential prey.

That was why Jelani Onyilogwu was far from his warm bed on such a cold night. He was on guard duty, kept warm by the cloth draped around him and the bundle of roasted yams his mother had given him before he'd left. When the tubers cooled, they would become nourishment for the long night ahead, but not before he absorbed as much of their radiant heat as possible.

He'd made himself a seat off the ground, both for comfort and for safety. Earlier rains made the ground muddy and drove snakes to the surface as their burrows flooded. He had no desire to be bitten by venomous serpents, but they weren't the only danger in the night.

It was relatively easy to drive away wild animals. Even a traveling elephant herd could be deterred with enough numbers and noise. All Jelani had to do was raise the alarm, and the village would come with lights, banging their pots and pans. Other humans, however, were a different beast. There was always the threat of thieves—the more prosperous the village, the bigger target it was.

The problem was exacerbated whenever there was unrest in neighboring Rwanda or Burundi. It happened with some regularity, even if the particulars were different each time. With thousands more mouths to feed, food and resources became even more precious.

Jelani had sympathy for the refugees that inundated Ngara from time to time. It wasn't that long ago that his family fled their ancestral home under threat of death. Tanzania had taken them in and provided shelter, food, water, clothing, and medical aid. Refugee camps looked like wretched places in media coverage, but the way his grandmother spoke of it, it was salvation.

When it came time for repatriation, his grandfather had successfully pleaded their case and they were allowed to stay and build a life in Tanzania. It wasn't perfect, but in their reckoning they stood a better chance of building a life in peace here, and each subsequent wave of refugees confirmed that belief. To Jelani, it only seemed right to extend the same courtesy to those that came after them, even though not all in his family felt that way.

Hungry refugees, robbers, and thieves were bad enough, but poachers were far and away the worst. They were ruthless and often heavily armed. Driven by the unquenchable demand for elephant tusks and rhinoceros' horns in Asia, poachers culled animals in unbelievable numbers. In recent years, the government clamped down on the illegal killing of wild animals and those that smuggled ivory and horns out of the country, but they couldn't be everywhere at once.

While the national anti-poaching units secured the nature preserves and game reserves, the poachers saw an opportunity in the corridors between them. There was 100 kilometers between the Burigi and Moyowosi Game Reserves, a route for elephants moving between the two protected areas. Jelani's village lay ten kilometers from the southern border of the Burigi Game Reserve and far from the two main roads that crossed the district—an ideal place for harvesting ivory.

He settled in but didn't dare get too comfortable. It would bring great dishonor to himself and his family to fall asleep on guard duty. The village relied on whoever kept watch because it allowed everyone else to get the rest for the hard work that waited for them in the morning. To stay awake, he would recite poems or stories in his head, do sums, or make up word games while he stared out into the fog and listened for intruders. He had a keen ear, which is how he heard the unnatural rustle among the foliage to the west.

"That better not be you, Faraji," he sternly spoke into the fog from which a familiar form sheepishly emerged.

"How did you know it was me?" the curious boy asked.

"Because everyone else has the good sense to stay in bed on a night like this," Jelani chided his younger brother. "You better go home before mama finds out you've gone."

"I don't want to go back," the twelve-year old petulantly objected. "Can't I stay out here with you and keep watch? I can help!" He held out his sling shot defiantly.

"You could, but then we would both get a beating," Jelani argued. He may have been a grown man, but his mother never was one to hold back on giving him a whooping when she felt it was deserved.

Faraji kicked at the dirt. "I'm not a kid anymore. I can do things."

Jelani heard the pride in his childish voice and tried a

different tactic. "I know that, little man. Why do you think I've asked you to go home? If something happens in the village while I'm out here, I'm counting on you to keep everyone safe."

Faraji considered his older brother's words. While Jelani's logic held up, he was still suspicious of his intent. "You're just saying that to trick me into returning."

Jelani shrugged and played it cool. "It doesn't matter why I'm saying it. It doesn't change the facts. If you are here, who is keeping them safe?" His sights were still on the fields, but he could see his younger brother working it out for himself in his peripheral vision.

"You promise not to tell mama I was out here?" Faraji tried to bargain his way out of trouble.

"If she doesn't already know, I don't see a reason to tell her," Jelani agreed.

The loud trumpet of elephants interrupted their negotiations. Faraji's eyes lit up at the promise of excitement. "I'll sound the alarm," he offered but Jelani abruptly stopped him with one hand and used the other to motion for him to stay quiet.

A few seconds later, the sound of rapid gunfire peppered the misty night. It wasn't just elephants out tonight, and even Faraji knew to stay quiet if poachers were about.

"Go back and tell *mjomba* Sahel there are poachers," Jelani whispered. Forewarned was forearmed, and if they tried to approach, the village would not be caught unaware. There was no objection or back talk from Faraji this time.

"What will you do?" he asked.

"Keep a watch on them. If they come this way, I'll try to steer them away or stall them," Jelani murmured. "Now go, before they get closer." Faraji nodded his head and disappeared into the fog, saying a prayer for his brother's safety as he ran.

# Chapter Five

Louisville, Kentucky, USA
2nd of May, 09:45 a.m. (GMT-4)

"Good morning, Louisville! Have you looked outside your window today? What a gorgeous day for the Derby! Blue skies are projected for the entire day, so be sure grab your sunscreen and hats before heading out to races. Current temperature is seventy-four degrees with highs in the mid-eighties.. Perfect weather to knock back a few mint juleps with friends. Don't forget to pick up your bottle of Woodford Reserve, the official bourbon—"

The radio cut out as Alan Brooks turned off the engine. He grabbed his bag and climbed out of his metallic gray Chevy Silverado. His sunglasses blocked out most of the sun, and the few clouds in the sky were white and fluffy, like cotton balls floating by in the light breeze. The morning DJ was right, it was a perfect day to spend at the track.

Brooks pulled a press badge from his bag and slung it around his neck as he neared the twin spires of Churchill Downs. The security guard checked his ID and credentials before letting him pass. The paddock was blissfully quiet and the only people crossing the grounds were staff associated with the track, the Derby, or a horse.

Not all horse races were created equal and the type of race required different skills of the horse and its jockey. In America, it was all about flat-track racing—a short, fast-paced sprint to the finish on a straight or oval track. The horses in any given contest were grouped by age, breed, gender, and performance to make the contest more competitive and exciting. Maiden races were only for those who had never won a race before, while claiming races were for horses up for sale that day.

The Kentucky Derby was a grade 1 stakes race, meaning none of the horses were for sale and the owners paid an entry fee for their three-year-old thoroughbreds to participate. It was a long road to become one of the final twenty, and all the horses were winners in their own right by the time they made it to Churchill Downs. The Run for the Roses was about finding the cream of the crop—the champion among champions—and only the winner of the Derby could hope to become an American Triple Crown.

While all the hoopla was centered on "The Most Exciting Two Minutes in Sports," it was, in fact, the final race of the day. The Paddock Gate opened for general admission at 10:00 a.m. with the first undercard's post time at 11:00. Once the hour turned, it wouldn't take long for the chaos to descend, especially with such nice weather. The eager would come early and claim their spots on the grass with blankets and folding chairs they had brought from home. Those in the infield couldn't even see the track; they paid to sit outside and watch the race on a giant screen branded the Big Board.

It might sound like foolish to some, but Brooks understood the urge to be near the action. Dangerously close to being mistaken for an old man, he'd spent a lifetime around horses. He'd even tried being a trainer in his youth but found he didn't have the disposition for it. What was good for the owners was not always good for the horses. He was too tall to be a jockey and too poor to be an owner, so he'd built a name for himself as a historian and horse profiler over the years.

The press corps was milling around the paddock, everyone simultaneously checking their phones and talking over each other. Every year, it got bigger and the journalists got younger. Brooks blamed the internet; these days, anyone could call themselves a correspondent if they had a registered website with enough advertisers.

He skirted the edge of the unruly mob and checked in with his boss—who was neither an editor nor magazine owner—via text to let her know he had arrived Although Brooks wrote articles for established periodicals to supplement his income, the bulk of his earnings came from private consulting. He'd learned long ago that the real money in horse racing took place off the track.

The sport of kings wasn't just about the size of the purse—easily over a million in the Derby—or which steed ran the fastest. Poor and rich alike played the horses. Last year's Kentucky Derby had a betting pool of $227 million spread across a card of fourteen races. Worldwide, wagering on horses was a $116 billion industry with the largest sectors in the US, UK, and Australia.

There was something for everyone. The risk averse choose safe bets that paid out less because losing hurt more than not winning very much. The dreamers went with the long odds with larger payouts because winning on a long shot felt like you were getting away with something. The handicappers tried to apply some logic to their picks, teetering somewhere between statistics and speculation. The hard-core gamblers placed wagers on any and every aspect of the race, finding exotic ways to scratch their itch. The betting establishment welcomed them all because no matter what bets were placed, they always took their vig.

When he started, he'd serviced a cadre of clients but time had paired it down to one: Angelica Zervo. She paid him very well for his insight and to make sure it was exclusively hers. She'd done well on the Oaks yesterday and was looking forward to hearing his recommendations for today's lineup.

There was an art to picking winners, and hitting the Daily Racing Form was just the beginning. Speed, past performance, previous winnings, and power stats—those were good points of data, but there was more to it than mathematics. There was the horse's temperament on the track, the caliber of the jockey, how much of a layoff it had before the race, and its position at the gate. If all those factors lined up just right, a long shot could take it all.

Brooks did his homework and crunched the numbers like any good handicapper, but whenever possible, he liked to see the horses the day of the race. That's where he picked up the unquantifiable factors—the weather, the track conditions, and the horses' dispositions.

Theoretically, anyone with a general admission ticket could see the horses on parade in the paddock, but in practice, it was nigh impossible with the crowds. Attendance could reach over 150,000 people on Derby Day, all jockeying for a peek at the horses before they took their position at the post. However, as a member of the press, Brooks would get access to the animals before and after the race, including a tour through the stables—a well-guarded area that was strictly closed to the public during the Derby.

But his press pass wasn't the only card up his sleeve. While everyone else looked for signs and portents in the paddock and consulted the animal's entourage about its condition, Brooks was getting it straight from the horse's mouth: all his life, he had a way with horses. They'd just understood each other.

He wasn't much of a magician otherwise. Outside of his work with animals he was pretty much a damp squib, barely able to even sense the supernatural. He thought of himself as a one-hit wonder, or a one-trick pony when he was feeling clever.

No practitioner could charm the horses—that was strictly prohibited by the people who covertly policed magic use in racing. But there was no rule against checking in on them and seeing how they felt right before the race, especially when no one else seemed to have his particular ability.

Brooks bided his time and reviewed his notes. In total, there were fourteen races today and the barns were packed. It was impossible for Brooks to get a read on all of them, but he'd perfected a system over the years.

He had his preliminary picks for all the races and focused his efforts on the main contenders of any given race. He generally ignored the longer odds unless he picked up something in passing that made him think a horse had the goods. While sports had a love affair with the Cinderella story, it rarely happened in reality. The next leg of the Triple Crown—Preakness Stakes in Baltimore, Maryland—only ran fourteen horses because eleventh was the best placement the six lowest ranking horses in the Derby ever got. By the time the Belmont Stakes were run, there were even fewer horses in the contest.

A stately woman came up the path and tried to call them to attention, but the cross talk drowned her out. She summoned a vocal bolt of lightning from behind her dimples and curls. "Members of the press, if I could have your attention!"

They fell quiet and turned to find the source of the voice. "I'm Marilyn Wilkes, media coordinator for today's event. Let me formally welcome you and thank you for being a part of

Derby Day. We have a full schedule. If you will follow me, we will start with a quick pass through the backside barns." She sashayed toward the security checkpoint and left the press corps to follow or get left behind.

As Brooks followed the pack, he listened with his will. Communicating with animals was harder than it looked, and anyone who has tried to have a conversation with their pet knew much was lost in translation. His initial impression was that the horses were unsettled. At first, he thought it was just normal racing day nerves. They were in an unfamiliar place surrounded by a lot of people and horses they did not know, not to mention the pressure everyone put on them. Their fortunes could change in the blink of an eye depending on how they performed today, and they knew it.

However, the uneasiness grew worse as he neared the section housing the Derby 20—like the spectator seats in the grandstand, stable placement was stratified by class. Something was wrong with the horses en masse, and he couldn't put his finger on it. His gut was roiling and it wasn't his ulcer.

While Ms. Wilkes paused to give Churchill Downs's official stance on the controversy of the day, Brooks approached one of the stalls whose collection of owners, trainers, jockeys, grooms, and veterinarians was momentarily absent. Lucky Lad was a chestnut with 7-2 odds in race 11, and Brooks shaped his will into something the horse would understand. *Hey buddy, what's got everyone so spooked?*

The thoroughbred turned his dark brown eyes on the practitioner and batted his long lashes. *Today, we run with death.*

Brooks had never known horses to speak metaphorically, but it wasn't like they were using words to communicate. It was more akin to playing telepathic charades. *Do you mean the horses are afraid of being put down if they don't do well?*

Lucky Lad snorted in what Brooks could only interpret as a cynical laugh. *Neigh, that is always so. Today, we run with our ancestor and death is never far behind.*

Brooks was fascinated at how calm this horse spoke of death and made some notes about pushing it up his ranking. He was about to make another salvo when a stablehand approached. "Can I help you?"

Brooks held up his lanyard. "Nope, just a member of the press admiring a horse."

"Better not let the owner or trainer catch you," the young man with the push broom cautioned. "Everyone's on pins and needles today."

Brooks eyed the name on his badge before replying. "Thanks for the warning, Mark, but I'm more afraid of her." He gestured to Wilkes, who was giving him the stink eye for wandering. The kid smirked but kept his head down as Brooks rejoined the pack and continued his recon.

Once the press corps was out of sight, the stablehand leaned his broom against the wall and reached into his pocket. He produced a carrot with one hand and coaxed the horse closer.

"Aren't you a pretty thing?" he crooned at a gray thoroughbred running in race 10. The horse stepped forward, enticed by the prospect of a treat. While the colt ate, the man dipped his thumb into the plastic bag of ash in his pocket and made a cross boxed in by a square on the horse's chest.

It was done by the time the carrot was consumed, and the horse and man went their separate ways. The young man wiped his thumb on a rag and took the broom in both hands. A smug smile crept across his face. He swept his way to his next target, whistling the chorus of "The Gambler."

# Chapter Six

Detroit, Michigan, USA
2nd of May, 6:21 p.m. (GMT-4)

The Kentucky Derby was ten furlongs, or one circuit plus an additional straightaway. It took the horses roughly two minutes to run it, with the current record at one minute and 59.4 seconds. Media coverage turned those two minutes into all-day coverage and brought the Kentucky Derby into homes and sports bars all over the world.

The viewers wanted an experience without having the benefit of being there. They couldn't smell Louisville in spring or the animals in the paddock. They couldn't hear the stands roar as they cheered for their horses or feel the ground move as the hooves beat on the dirt track. Fortunately, the networks were all too willing to manufacture the emotional stakes and excitement from afar in exchange for premium advertising dollars.

They had commentators in the studio and correspondents live at the track, passing the baton back and forth to keep their audience engaged. They aired the other races leading up to the main event and filled the time between runs with stats and projections from the analysts. For those less interested in the numbers side, there were plenty of celebrity spottings, shots of audacious hats, and other premade race-adjacent segments.

There were lots of long pans of Louisville and Churchill Downs with flowery exposition voiced over soaring instrumentals. Every year, they put together a retrospective that touched on the history of the race with old pictures to connect the present to the past. With twenty contenders, there was plenty of fodder in each individual horse's road to the Derby and how they stacked up against the competition. If none of them had a particularly inspirational story, they could always revisit past Triple Crown winners and recount their ascent from past Derbies. Between segments, there were plenty of commercial breaks for suburbanites holding Derby parties to refill their mint juleps and nibble on Benedictine sandwiches and country ham biscuits.

Leader always kept tabs on the races. It was one of the creative ways she stretched the off-books money received from the CIA and FBI to operate the Salt Mine. When it looked like nothing pressing would keep them at work this weekend, Chloe suggested making a day of it. Dot and Leader were less than enthusiastic about the idea, but the crafty librarian skillfully addressed their objections. She bribed her sister with her favorite foods and pledged to keep it an intimate gathering in town in case something came up.

Leader went along with the charade, which is how she

found herself sipping a mint julep in Meridiana's living room wearing a paper hat she'd made earlier that afternoon. It was just the four of them, women whose history together had been long and interwoven. There was no need to use assumed names or pretend to be anything other than their true selves.

Chloe and Dot came out of the kitchen with a generous slice of Derby pie in each hand before reclaiming their spot on the couch. "Did we miss anything?" Chloe asked before handing a plate to Leader.

"No, we're still watching the horses walk from the barn to the paddock," Meridiana answered before taking a slice from Dot. As a succubus she got no nourishment from it, but of all the foods she'd tried during her time among mortals, she loved chocolate the best, one of the key ingredients of the classic dessert along with chopped walnuts and bourbon. Culinary speaking, it was the closest she got to being sinful ever since she was cursed to do no evil and forced to give up consuming souls.

Leader had had a good day at the races so far, winning three out of four bets on average although some were wider than others. Brooks always gave his strongest recommendations when he'd communicated with the horses, and she would place tighter bets on those races. Horses backed purely from handicapping were always qualified, and she would bet wide to increase her chances of winning, but historically, they were the least performing financially. Of course, Brooks had no idea that

Angelica Zervo was, in fact, the head of the Salt Mine and one of the most-fearsome magicians in the world.

He strongly recommended his pick for the Derby even though the horse's odds were 10 to 1, meaning if they held the race eleven times, the horse was expected to lose ten times. She'd placed a Win on it because his magical ability rarely led her astray. As she waited for the final race to start, she couldn't shake the feeling that something wasn't right and it nagged at her.

"Penny for your thoughts, Pen?" Meridiana asked when she noticed the salt- and pepper-haired woman hadn't yet touched her pie.

The diffuse haze in Leader's gray eyes came into focus as she nailed down what was bothering her. "What are the odds of none of the top three favorites winning thirteen races in a row?"

Her companions knew that tone and tried to pull her back into the festive mood. "I've had too many mint juleps to do the math," the succubus joked.

Dot's blue eyes narrowed. "Di, you don't get drunk on alcohol."

"No, but it doesn't make doing math more fun either," she drily remarked. "This is a nice, Chloe," she tried to change the subject.

"Thanks! It's the original recipe. Only me and the Kern family know it," she boasted. "And Dot, if she ever paid any attention while I was making it."

"Division of labor," Dot spoke up with a mouth full of gooey goodness.

"It's got to be one in the billions," Leader persisted, counting up all the zeros. Either all the betting houses got it wrong, or something was afoot.

"Let's just call it damn near close to impossible and watch the big race," Meridiana suggested.

"Right, of course," Leader replied and took a bite of pie. "Oh Chloe, this really is good." The right half of the conjoined twins beamed with pride. They watched the parade of horses as they waited for "Riders Up"—the call for jockeys to mount their horses and move to the track. "I'm just going to make a call," Leader said as she put her plate next to her drink on the coffee table.

Dot groaned. "You are the worst! Only you could be dissatisfied with *all those winnings*."

"It's not the winning that bother me. It's the *winners*," she said emphatically. "Not a single one from the top of the pack? You have to admit that is questionable," she reasoned.

Meridiana stayed out of it and focused on her dessert, but the twins begrudgingly agreed—they'd had to stop their drinking game because of the number of times the commentators said the words *storybook*, *Cinderella*, or *fairytale*. "You think your inside man is responsible?" Chloe asked.

"My guy?" Leader said incredulously. "No, I don't think he

has the skill or imagination to pull something like this off."

"But you think someone is picking the winners," Meridiana spoke her old friend's suspicions out loud.

"Why can't it just be plain old doping?" Dot said wistfully. She could smell more work coming her way.

"If it were one or two underdogs, maybe. But all of them?" Leader posited the question rhetorically as she rose and pulled out her phone. "Just one quick call and I'll be back before they finish singing 'My Old Kentucky Home.'"

As she dashed into the bathroom for privacy, the other three women resumed their merry making. They were well versed with the ebb and flow of history to appreciate the utter luxury of idle chatter. They had almost made it through a whole gathering without losing Leader to work, but at least she came—that was progress.

Leader closed the door behind her and took off her hat before dialing. Her powers of concentration were nonpareil, but even she couldn't help being distracted by her reflection in the mirror. Seeing herself in a paper plate hat bedecked with construction paper rosebuds was too ridiculous. She summoned her will and her eyes took on a new depth and sharpness.

The line picked up on the third ring. "Hello?" Brooks answered over the background noise.

"Mr. Brooks, this is Ms. Zervo," she spoke, enrobing each syllable she uttered in a sheet of her will. "I know you've already made your picks, but I'd like you to stick around after the race and get close to the winners. See if there is any change in the horses since this morning."

Suddenly, all his plans of cutting out early and beating the traffic vanished. How she knew he spoke to horses didn't cross his mind in this moment of singular clarity. All he knew was that he needed to stay and check on the horses.

"Sure," he readily agreed. "Anything for my best client."

She smiled. "I'm your only client, Mr. Brooks."

"Exactly," he answered in the call and response they had developed over the years.

"We'll talk later this evening. Enjoy the main event, Mr. Brooks," she signed off. He didn't have a chance to respond before she ended the call.

She quickly dialed a second number, this one to the analysts on the third floor of the Salt Mine. She requested a flag on people that won on the Derby's main race that had also won in additional races earlier in the day. When in doubt, follow the money.

With the wheels in motions, she'd done enough to calm the itch that had been building with each unlikely winning wager. Leader positioned her hat back on her head and tied the ribbon under her chin. They had made the party small and away from the S&M dungeon at 18 is 9 to accommodate her. The least she could do was try to have a good time.

She emerged from the bathroom in a lighter mood and Meridiana called out, "Penny, you gotta see this. I do believe we have a winner for most hideous hat. Hurry before they pan away!"

It was an unfortunate shade of pale blue and green and at least three feet tall. There must have been yards of gauzy material, stiffened and wrapped into impossible origami. It sparkled dynamically with each head movement as different sewn-in sequins caught the light. For some inexplicable reason, it also had feathers. The cameraman must have agreed with them, because he lingered upon the monstrosity like a stage actor savoring every syllable of the best line in the play.

"I'm pretty sure you could see that from space," Chloe declared.

"Someone needs to tell that poor woman bigger isn't always better," Leader added as she took her seat and picked up what was left of her slice of pie. "The sad thing is that that hat probably cost a fortune, which is why fashion is complete bullshit."

"I don't know. The world is looking at her and talking about her...isn't that the point of fashion?" Meridiana conjectured with a sly smile before starting on her second piece.

"Maybe she was going for peacock meets cotton candy," Chloe said charitably.

Dot shook her head disdainfully. "Cleanse it with fire. It's the only way to be sure."

# Chapter Seven

Mark Kinkade gave his dashboard a good slap and the intermittent rattling stopped. His old beater wasn't exactly reliable, but it was paid for and it hadn't fallen apart. Yet. He'd always said as soon as he could afford it, he would stop sinking money into repairing his truck and buy something new. He wasn't looking for a luxury vehicle and he wouldn't be caught dead in a vanity SUV, but a reliable work truck would be nice. He smiled widely…tomorrow, he'd start looking.

As he cruised down the highway, he was making a list of what he could do with his winnings. Kinkade was a cautious man by nature; earlier today, he'd only bet a portion of his cash reserves in case of failure. Would smudging a little ash on horses really work?

Even as he placed his final wager, he'd harbored a sliver of doubt. Sure, the handful of other horses he'd bet on earlier had won, but he didn't want to get his hopes up. He was like Charlie Brown, and life was Lucy with that cursed football. He was pretty sure he was going to end up on his ass again, but he had to keep kicking. Damned if he didn't make contact this time. He'd stayed long enough to see a garland of roses draped around his horse's neck in the winner's circle. He wanted to make sure it was real and not just a dream.

It felt good to be a winner and he couldn't help but calculate what his winnings would have been if he'd betted it all. It was the easiest money he'd ever made. It would have taken decades of saving to earn that kind of scratch. There would be plenty of time to make budgets and figure out how much to put aside, but tonight was about celebrating—steak dinners, top shelf booze, and cigars all around. He'd always wanted to be the guy that bought a round for everyone in the bar.

But first, he had to clean up, feed the dog, and wait for his buddy to get off work. Having money wasn't any fun without having someone to share it with, and it would be nice to be the one picking up the bill for a change.

He exited the highway and drove into Parkland, a run-down working-class neighborhood that was dying on the vine. He'd inherited his grandparents' house a few years ago, and the ranch-style home of his house-proud gram and gramps had also seen better days. They had let things slide in their later years and he did what he could, but even materials cost something.

He pulled under the carport and his headlights spotlighted the faded and chipped siding. Last year, he'd priced out what it would cost to replace if he did the labor himself. At the time, it was well beyond his budget.

A strange sort of euphoria came over him as it dawned on him that he had the means to fix it properly. *Is this how rich people feel all the time?* he wondered as he pulled the keys out of the ignition.

He fished the right key from the ring and opened the front door. "Baxter, I'm home. I did good today! No more generic dry food for you, buddy," he called out, expecting to hear the jingle of his tags. He tossed his keys on the sideboard and bent down to scoop up the mail that had passed through the slot. "Baxter, where are you, boy?" he called out into the silence. Usually he'd be tripping over the burly furball by now.

He switched on the light in the living room and checked the dog bed next to the well-worn recliner that had belonged to his grandfather. When he found it empty, he muttered to himself, "Where did that dog get to?"

Baxter was a bon fide mutt he'd rescued from the pound with his last serious girlfriend. The girl left but Baxter stayed, which was fine by Kinkade as the canine was a hellava lot more faithful than she'd ever been. It wasn't like him to wander at night, but the doggie door in the kitchen granted him the freedom to roam while Kinkade was at work.

He took a seat in the recliner and started unlacing his boots. It was the sort of thing his grandmother and ex-girlfriend would have frowned upon—wearing his work boots into the house—but there was no one to fuss about dragging dirt inside now. He was thinking about what it would cost to replace the threadbare carpet with hardwood laminate when he heard the tinkling of dog tags knocking against each other in the kitchen. Figures—wherever Baxter had gotten to, he'd always return when he got hungry. "There you are, boy!" he greeted his returning friend.

Kinkade was still hunched over when he heard the connecting door swing on its hinges. "Just let me get these boots off and I'll get you some dinner." He caught the furry form lumbering toward him in his periphery. That was why he was a dog person—Baxter was always excited to see him.

He'd just taken off his second boot when the dog jumped onto his lap. Kinkade gave his dog a vigorous petting with both hands but pulled away when he made contact with the sticky mess on his tawny fur. It was too sticky to be mud but it was dark and smelled earthy. "What have you been rolling in, boy?" he chastised him and tried to dislodge the big dog from his lap. "Looks like both of us need a bath."

Baxter pressed harder and stayed put, nosing his way closer. "I missed you too buddy, but we gotta get you cleaned up," he tried to reason with his dog. "This is definitely backyard hose worthy."

Kinkade knew something was very wrong when he looked into Baxter's eyes. There was no warmth or recognition there, no trace of the sweet-tempered dog he'd come to know and love. Instead of the big brown eyes that always convinced him to give the mutt an extra treat, there was endless blackness.

"What the hell?!" Kinkade exclaimed, but it was too late. Baxter's powerful jaws clamped down on Kinkade's throat and his sharp canines tore into the soft, exposed flesh. Warm sanguine rivers drained from the veins while the pressurized blood spurted from the arteries. The dog kept hold of his prize despite Kinkade's flailing. When the body stilled and slumped in the recliner, Baxter let go. His furry form stepped off the furniture and padded back into the kitchen.

# Chapter Eight

Matumaini Village, Ngara District, Kagera, Tanzania
3rd of May, 10:05 a.m. (GMT+3)

The Toyota Land Cruiser cut ruts into the muddy ground as it ventured deeper into the countryside, jostling its passengers with every divot and rock that passed beneath its wheels. An elephant killed by poachers wasn't anything new, but when the poachers were also found dead, it complicated matters.

Yazid Alaneme couldn't decline when the regional director of the Department of Natural Resources and Tourism called him into work on a Sunday. He reassured his wife that God would understand and if He didn't, all the more reason she should go to church without him and pray for his soul.

The driver knew the area well but made sure to follow the coordinates with Alaneme on board. He knew they were close when he saw the crowd of people gathered in the middle of nowhere. Members of the local anti-poaching unit were already on site, and they waved down the vehicle and shouted at the spectators to make way.

The guards were armed and organized, but even they couldn't keep all the gawkers at bay. Word of the gruesome scene had spread faster than a wildfire, and the tarp covering the bodies only added fuel to the flames. They saluted when Alaneme got out of the vehicle, which put the locals on alert—someone of importance had arrived.

Alaneme did a quick assessment of the scene. A lone bull elephant lay dead with one of his tusks recently removed and the other still attached. There was another vehicle parked nearby, presumably the poachers'. A large sheet of plastic covered the poachers' bodies, weighted down with rocks along the edge.

He put on his game face—that of a stern but paternal figure. "Everyone, please go home. We need to conduct a thorough investigation here and that is not possible with so many extra people moving about. I need to speak to the person or persons who discovered the scene, but everyone else needs to leave. Now." There was no ambiguity in Alaneme's serious demeanor; he meant business.

The crowd thinned as people slowly dispersed, reluctantly abandoning any hope of catching a glimpse of what was under the sheet. Eventually, only two locals remained: a young man in his late teens to early twenties and an older man in his forties.

Alaneme addressed them collectively. "You two discovered the bodies?"

The older man stepped forward. "My nephew did, sir, but his mother asked me to be present."

"And you are?"

"Sahel Onyilogwu," he replied with a slight bow.

Alaneme turned to the other. "What is your name, young man?"

"Jelani Onyilogwu, sir," he answered, mimicking his uncle in deference but he couldn't keep the tremor out of his voice.

Alaneme took off his sunglasses and adopted a less imposing stance. "Tell me what happened, Jelani."

"I was keeping watch on the fields two nights ago when I heard an elephant call followed by gunfire. I sent my younger brother back to tell my uncle poachers were in the area."

"What time was this?"

Jelani hesitated. "I'm not sure. I didn't have a watch, but it was nine when I left the house and I had been out there a while."

"His brother came to me a little after eleven," Sahel backed up his nephew.

Alaneme's eyebrow raised. "Why isn't your younger brother here?"

"He's at home as punishment. He wasn't supposed to be out that night," Jelani explained.

"Ah," Alaneme uttered. He knew how quickly a mother's worry turned to wrath once she knew her naughty child was safe. "Go on."

"I went toward the gunfire—" he continued.

"Why on earth did you do that?" his interrogator cut him off.

"I wanted to see where they were and make sure they didn't

approach the village," he said weakly.

Alaneme looked to Sahel and the men shared a look—the foolhardy nature of youth. "That was very brave, but very foolish," he cautioned the young man.

"I understand that now, sir," Jelani accepted the criticism. It wasn't the first time such had been said to him in the past day.

Alaneme continued, "What did you observe when you got closer?"

"There were three men. I heard them arguing. One was complaining that they only found one elephant while another was thankful it was a mature male with big tusks. The third told both of them to quit talking and help him with the cutting," Jelani reported faithfully.

"What language were they speaking?" he inquired. There were over a hundred different languages spoken in Tanzania, and if the poachers were speaking a tribal or regional language, it could help the authorities track down their identity.

"Swahili, sir," Jelani answered. Swahili was a blend of Bantu and Arabic and was the national language that was taught in primary school—it shed no light on who the poachers were or where they came from.

"The elephant still has one of his tusks. Did you see what interrupted the poachers?"

"Not clearly. It was very foggy, but I saw something charge them. There was a lot of screaming, yelling, and gunfire until it took down all three."

Alaneme considered what predators hunted nocturnally in these parts. "A pride of lions?"

Jelani shook his head. "No. There was just one and it was the wrong shape to be a lion. It looked like a zebra, only taller, with no stripes."

Alaneme nodded but the men from the anti-poaching unit looked at each other incredulously—they had never heard of a lone zebra attacking three armed men. "What happened next?"

The young man's eyes glazed over, replaying what could not be unseen. "It stepped on their bodies—I could hear their bones breaking. Then it…it started eating them, sir."

Alaneme said nothing and approached the tarp. It was dirty and battered, creased from years of repeated use. He removed a rock and lifted an edge. The smell was overwhelming but not as horrific as the sight of it. It was a bloody mess; the chest cavity was open and the ribs punched in. He heard one of the men behind him start to wretch but he kept his face stoic.

"Who covered the bodies?" he asked as he let the tarp drop and replaced the rock.

Sahel spoke, "I did that, sir. When Jelani returned to the village, I had him show me the location so I could notify the authorities. I thought it best. The bodies were…unnatural." He and Alaneme shared another look, this one more probative.

"Did you touch anything or remove anything from the scene otherwise?" Alaneme grilled him.

"No, sir," Sahel said firmly.

Alaneme turned to Jelani. "What about you?"

"No, sir," the young man adamantly answered.

Alaneme straightened his posture and clothing before delivering his official remarks. "Thank you for doing your civic duty. Poachers are a menace to everyone, not just the animals. You may return to your village. We know where it is if we have further questions. Once our people have removed the bodies, I'll have someone return your tarp."

The two locals nodded but Sahel respectfully objected. "That is very thoughtful, but it is an old tarp. Better to destroy it when you are finished with it. We've needed a new one anyway."

Alaneme nodded. He felt it, too. Something…unnatural. Unfortunately, this wasn't the first time he'd seen such things—other human remains with similar injuries had been recently found between the Burigi and Moyowosi Game Reserves. Something was feeding in the corridor, and it didn't eat wild game.

Alaneme issued a string of orders as Jelani and his uncle walked away: photograph the scene, take a thorough inventory of the poachers' possessions, and collect the corpses for medical examination. While the men were busy with their assigned tasks, he stole away to make a phone call.

The line rang three times before someone answered. "Institute of Tradition, preserving cultures around the globe.

How may I direct your call?"

"Yes, this is Yazid Alaneme of the East Africa branch. I would like to leave a message for one of your correspondents about a possible story for the next edition."

# Chapter Nine

Teresa Martinez walked through the lone terminal of the Louisville International Airport with her Salt Mine standard issue carryon rolling along beside her. She had no doubt that Moncrief's metallic cobalt G650 was parked somewhere on the tarmac, but that wasn't how she'd arrived. She had flown commercial, albeit in business class—the only seats left when her ticket was booked. At five feet ten, the extra leg room did not go unappreciated, even on such a brief flight.

Martinez was no stranger to air travel between her stint at the Bureau and her year and a half at the Salt Mine, and she was certain this modest airport was international by technicality only. It was a title granted to ports of entry that could accept cargo from other countries even if there were no international passenger flights. Municipalities leaned hard into the words "international airport" because it raised perceptions and they hoped that made them an international city in people's eyes.

While some airports favored glass and steel or every shade of gray, SDF was an homage to beige with every color from ecru to taupe splashed on the floors, walls, and ceiling. The shops and eateries in the circular atrium were open for business, albeit sluggish this morning. Like the rest of Louisville, they were still hungover from last night's revelry.

Despite the general stupor, heads still turned as Martinez passed. Her heels marked time with each click on the speckled linoleum floor and the folds of her burgundy dress swished around her long legs as she sauntered down the concourse, following the signs to car rentals.

She stopped at the counter and rang the bell for service, flashing the attendant a warm smile. It was slim pickings with the city at peak tourism capacity, but there was always a rental car available, usually a high-end luxury sedan. Most people regarded cars as a necessary utility and opted to spend their money on other aspects of their vacation: staying at a fancier hotel, eating out at nicer places, doing more shopping, or drinking without regard to the tab. Those that found value in driving expensive cars invariably picked sports cars. Luxury rental sedans weren't sexy or fun, but they were almost always available. At least they all had smooth rides.

It was a short drive to her destination, a four-star hotel in the middle of Downtown Louisville. Although it was Derby weekend and the hotels were fully booked, Moncrief always kept one standing suite available at each of her family's extensive holdings. They weren't gauche enough to emblazon the Moncrief name on the building, but anyone in the know knew the establishment was one of theirs.

The red-carpet treatment didn't start until Martinez stopped by the desk for a room key; she couldn't even get on the floor of the suite Moncrief was staying in without one. Once she said Alicia's name, staff came out of the woodwork to assist her. They had been informed that Ms. Moncrief was expecting a guest this morning, but they were clearly not expecting someone like Martinez.

She had already parked the car and wouldn't need valet. She only had one small piece of luggage that she could manage herself. An escort to the room was unnecessary—the key and the wifi code would suffice. Martinez had traveled with Moncrief before and understood their confusion. With each polite but firm dismissal of aid, it slowly sunk in that she was also a visitor into Moncrief's social sphere.

When she got to the room, she knocked on the door instead of letting herself in with the key. She heard Moncrief's voice on the other side and her bubbly disposition spilled through the doorway as she opened it. "Well, aren't you a tall drink of water!" Her tone was light and smile bright, but her eyes switched from socialite to co-conspirator when she recognized a fellow agent.

"I clean up all right, when the occasion calls for it," Martinez replied as they exchanged two kisses on alternating cheeks to keep up appearances. "Thanks for putting me up. There isn't an empty bed for miles."

"No problem. Come in and put your things away," Moncrief graciously opened the door wider.

Martinez's hazelnut eyes scanned the room from behind her impeccable smoky eye treatment. The suite was enormous and the remains of breakfast were still on the dining nook. She paused at the carafe. "Is there any coffee left?"

Moncrief waved flippantly as she closed the door. "Help yourself. I'm almost ready."

Martinez brushed her wavy chestnut hair over her shoulder and poured herself a cup. It wasn't quite fresh but it was still warm. Moncrief sat at the vanity in her silk robe and resumed putting on her makeup. "You want to tell me why Leader called me late last night to get an invitation for two to the winners' brunch?"

Martinez took another sip before setting her cup down and opening her luggage. "She thinks someone or something fixed the races yesterday and she wants me to take a look around the stables and the horses before everyone leaves the city," she replied as she opened the concealed compartment in her suitcase. She was fine with packing her navy suit and sensible shoes for later, but there was no way she was going in without her Glock 43, even if her ensemble required creative positioning.

Moncrief put down her mascara wand and frowned a little. "Well, I could have done that."

"There is also a dead body in the morgue to look into," Martinez added as she pulled out the Glock. "Mark Kinkade,

Churchill Downs's employee who started yesterday with a thousand dollars in wagers that became nearly six figures after he'd rolled his five undercard winnings into his Derby bet. He was found dead in his home later that night." As she shared the details of her woefully thin briefing, her hands moved automatically, reassembling the gun and doing a mechanical check.

"Well that isn't at all suspicious," Moncrief remarked sarcastically as she painted her pale lashes. "So what's the plan?"

"Poke around Churchill Downs with an emphasis on the horses, then I'll stop by the dead man's house afterward to see if there is anything to investigate," she answered, holstering her weapon and strapped it high on her right thigh. Although there wasn't much for the analysts to pull from the Louisville PD database about Kinkade's death, his remains were sitting in the city morgue and she had his home address. If there were no traces of magic or the supernatural, she'd be back in Detroit by Tuesday at the latest.

"I'm not sure what Leader hopes you'll find. All practitioners know Churchill Downs takes extreme measures to prevent magical interference and enchantments. All the big tracks do," Moncrief objected before she traced her lips and filled them in rosy pink.

"Security systems and safes never stop thieves from trying," Martinez argued as she checked her own makeup and hair in the mirror before taking a seat to finish her coffee.

Moncrief conceded the point with a slight bob of her head as she rubbed her lip together and blotted. There was a long tradition of lucky charms, miracle salves, and pre-race rituals in horse racing, and it only got worse with people who knew magic was real. The challenge of sneaking something past the gatekeepers constituted its own sport. She rose from the table and walked to the closet. "Do you want to come in as FBI or a different alias?"

Martinez finished her cup and gave it some thought. "Let's stick with Tracy Martin from the Institute of Tradition. If being FBI comes up later, the story is that I write under a pen name to keep my personal life separate from work. You can decide if you knew or not."

Moncrief mentally started constructing the scaffolding around today's performance. "I knew but didn't say," she said thoughtfully before switching her tone and demeanor. "We never know when we will need a connection in federal law enforcement." Martinez smirked at the royal we. The Moncriefs were as close to magical royalty as one could get in North America.

The heiress slipped out of her robe and stepped into her dress—a Philo original soutache sheath dress with sheer flutter sleeves. She turned around and motioned for an assist. "What do you know about horses?"

Martinez obliged and zipped her up. "I think I got a My Little Pony as a birthday gift once," she answered honestly.

Moncrief laughed out loud, but it was more bemused than mean-spirited. "That's okay. We'll lean into it. Rich people love talking about themselves by way of their hobbies. If you admittedly know nothing, it gives them an excuse to 'educate' you."

Moncrief put on her jewelry and filled in Martinez on her end. "We are dining with Team Tall Boy, the surprise winner of the fourth race. He's owned by Justin Peterson, new money by way of the tech sector. He's definitely *not* a practitioner, but that doesn't mean someone working with the horse isn't."

"And he's easy on the eyes?" she surmised by Moncrief's thirsty expression.

"Absolutely gorgeous until his opens his mouth," Moncrief lamented. She eyed the plunging neckline of Martinez's Grecian-style dress and the bronze glow from their girls' weekend in Greece last month. "You're just his type, so I have no doubt we can wrangle an invitation to see the victorious stud."

"Too much for Sunday brunch?" Martinez feigned innocence. She had picked the dress because the skirt was full enough for her to strap a concealed weapon to her thigh, but in her experience, more cleavage never hurt in the field of social engagement.

"Nonsense," Moncrief dismissed the notion. "It will shake things up, and the rich are so amused by the antics of the masses," she said with a heavy dose of satirical sarcasm. "Just be yourself and they will be charmed at the novelty."

They did a final gear check before leaving the room, and as soon as they crossed the threshold they became two women on their way to brunch. "Have you ever had a hot brown sandwich?" Moncrief gaily asked as they entered the elevator.

"I can't say that I have," Martinez answered the query like it was a matter of grave importance.

Moncrief pantomimed surprise and delight. "Well, you're in for a treat!"

# Chapter Ten

Louisville, Kentucky, USA
3rd of May, 11:35 a.m. (GMT-4)

There were many dining opportunities at the track during the Derby to accommodate all echelons of visitors—the more expensive the price tag, the better the ambience and view. Everyone wanted to feel like they were part of something exclusive, and Churchill Downs delivered. Regardless on which level they dined, there was always someone they could look down upon from their perch.

However, there was one meal where attendance could not be bought: the Sunday winners' brunch. Only the top horses' owners were in attendance and, of course, their guests. The stolid dining room was abuzz with heady energy when Moncrief and Martinez entered. Given the number of long shots that won purses yesterday, spirits were higher than usual, last night's celebration notwithstanding. The best cure for a hangover was another drink and it was never too early for mimosas.

The two women played out their charade while conducting surveillance. The cheerful heiress led her wide-eyed guest around the room to see and be seen, sprinkling a little of her social capital as they circulated. Martinez was too experienced and long in the tooth to be a true ingénue, but she took plenty of pictures and video along the way to sell how novel she found it all.

Unbeknownst to those in the background, Martinez periodically created an auditory prestidigitation that was only perceptible to practitioners. It was a fast and dirty way to screen many people for possible suspects should they uncover evidence of magical interference. Anyone who reacted to the noise was of interest.

Moncrief skillfully orchestrated their path to end at Team Tall Boy's table, where four men sat with drinks in hand. A man with glasses was in heated discussion with a thoroughly tanned blond. A slim, dark-haired man watched bemused while the fourth nursed his drink. Martinez rightly pegged the last man as Peterson, as he was the only one that could qualify as "absolutely gorgeous" even if he wasn't her type.

"Incoming," she warned Moncrief in a low murmur. The heiress fixed her smile and waved to them as Martinez made the sound of dishes breaking en masse just behind the table. None of them flinched at the sound and the handsome one with sandy brown hair and saturated blue eyes rose at their approach. "Alicia, how good of you to join us. I was about to send out a search party," he drolly greeted her.

"Don't be a bore, Justin," she replied with kiss on the cheek. "I just wanted to show Tracy around." It was unclear whether her guest was being given a tour or was in fact an object on display, but either could be believed given her delivery. Moncrief found it was easier to be everything to everyone if there was room for interpretation.

"If you clip a butterfly's wings they cannot fly away, but you damage the most beautiful part of them," the spectacled man at the table spoke metaphorically before rising and introducing himself with a slight nod. "Miles Henderson of Equus International."

"Alicia Moncrief," she reciprocated, even though it was clear everyone knew who she was. "And this is my friend, Tracy Martin."

Martinez smiled sweetly and addressed Peterson. "Thanks for the invitation. I've never been to the Derby, much less the winners' brunch. It's quite a view," she alluded to the panoramic windows.

"Yes, it is," he agreed, scanning Martinez in his periphery. "Forgive my manners. You've already met Miles, Tall Boy's breeder. This is Ian McGonagall, his trainer," he gestured to the blond. "And Jack Hennessy, his rider." The jockey was seated with his back to a pillar: he raised his dark eyes and glass to the women but declined to stand.

As they took their seats, Martinez found herself between the jockey and the trainer while Moncrief sat opposite her next to Peterson and Henderson. The seating immediately told the agents where everyone on Team Tall Boy was in the hierarchy.

Peterson motioned to the waiter. "Another round of mimosas for the table," he ordered.

"Certainly, sir. Would you like to order your meal at this time?" the waiter inquired.

"I was told I had to try a hot brown," Martinez answered in hopes of eating sooner rather than later. Breakfast had been hours ago back in Detroit and she was famished.

"I *do* like a hot brown," Peterson said suggestively. The table was split between cringing at the clumsy innuendo and chuckling at the unintended scatological overtones. Martinez groaned internally at the terrible come on but kept the neutral smile plastered on her face. He was their ticket into the stables.

"What's not to love about a turkey, bacon, and cheese sandwich smothered in a Mornay sauce?" Moncrief asked rhetorically in an effort to cut through the creepiness. "I'll have the same," she added brightly.

After everyone placed their order, Martinez directed the conversation toward the Derby. "Alicia tells me it was quite a day at the races. I'm sorry I missed it."

Peterson beamed with pride. "I knew Tall Boy had the goods," he said with aplomb.

"Of course! He was bred to be a winner," Henderson asserted.

"Bollocks," McGonagall declared with a slight lilt. "Genetics is a crapshoot. What really counts is the training. That's where you cultivate the traits of a champion."

"We aren't putting two horses together in a stall and leaving things to chance," Henderson objected and reflexively straightened his glasses. "There's a whole science to it."

Hennessy scoffed at the bickering men. "You can plot and plan all you like behind the scenes but on the big day, it's just me and the animal on the track. You want to get the best out of a horse? Put a good jockey on his back."

Martinez and Moncrief coordinated across the table with their eyes to make the most of the tension as each tried to claim the largest responsibility for the victory as their own. Martinez cleared her throat and raised her pitch a little higher than normal. "I don't know much about racing, but doesn't Tall Boy's win prove you're all at the top of your game? The horse included," she added at the last minute. Tempers calmed and the face-saving began—it was bad form to bicker in front of a novice who had no hopes of understanding the complexities of the argument.

"An astute observation, Tracy," Peterson complimented. "Where did you find her, Alicia?" His tone held more surprise than was flattering, but Martinez accepted it gracefully and gave Moncrief a look. She was right—he was becoming noticeably less attractive with every utterance.

"You know me, Justin. I have a knack for finding interesting people," she replied vaguely. She casually segued to their end target. "I don't suppose you could arrange a stop by the barns after brunch? I feel bad that Tracy missed the races and seeing a winner up close is the next best thing."

Peterson gave her an oily grin. "I would like nothing better…but Miles and I have meetings after this. I've got a thoroughbred to stud," he crowed.

"You could accompany me," McGonagall offered. "I wanted to check in on Tall Boy before we left town."

Martinez's face lit up. "That would be great," she enthusiastically replied to seal the deal.

Moncrief raised an eyebrow. "Is everything okay with Tall Boy?"

Peterson shot the trainer a menacing look—even the hint of injury could cast aspersions during crucial negotiations. McGonagall quickly downplayed his concern and leaned into his Irish accent. "Just a minor skin issue; nothing my special salve won't fix," he said with a wink.

"Tall Boy is bred for speed and strength. A little rash won't take him down," Henderson dismissed the trainer as a mother hen. "His job now is to sire more winners." He directed his attention to Moncrief, "Do you have any interest in investing? I'm sure I could find you a worthy steed or two."

"You're barking up the wrong tree, Miles," Peterson taunted him. "Alicia is only a spectator of equestrian sports."

"It's true," she confirmed. "I spend more on fun hats than in betting slips. But it's good to know I have someone to turn to if I change my mind," she turned him down gently. She didn't like to close doors because she never knew when someone would become useful later.

When the waiter returned with a tray of mimosas, Moncrief made a toast. "To Team Tall Boy…congratulations on a brilliant race!"

"Here, here," Peterson concurred and raised his glass. The flukes clinked around the table and it only took a taste for Martinez to figure out they didn't skimp on the champagne and the orange juice wasn't from concentrate. She made a mental note to go on assignment with Clover more often as she took another sip.

The table broke into private conversation as they waited for their food. Henderson and McGonagall continued their nature versus nurture debate, albeit in a more collegial tone, while Peterson tried to wrangle an invitation to Carmarthen for the Preakness Stakes. A stay at the Moncrief family home would certainly raise his standing with the old money that liked to look down their noses at him.

Unfortunately for him, Moncrief was a pro at avoiding social traps and had a way of saying no to people that made it seem like it was their idea all along. It was watching a puppet show, but he had no idea she was pulling his strings.

As they would have plenty of time to get information out of the trainer at the barns, Martinez turned to the quiet man beside her. "Hennessy—any affiliation to the distillery?"

"Sadly, no. My parents named me after their favorite things. My mother favors whisky and my father, himself," he joked with a self-deprecating grin.

She chuckled at his punch line, and her warm laugh chipped away at his gruff exterior. He wasn't in his element, but there was no way he was going to pass on the winners' brunch. He basked in the pleasure of amusing a pretty woman and his demeanor relaxed as he warmed up to her.

"And what brings you to fair Louisville in the company of the illustrious Alicia Moncrief?" His turn of phrase told Martinez how to approach.

"Traveling for work. I write for a publication funded by one of her pet projects," she replied, matching his mood.

"You're a writer!" he exclaimed. Most of the attractive plus ones at these things were not selected for their intellect. "Anything I might have read?"

She shrugged. "Probably not. I mostly write freelance and it's more famine than feast at the moment. However, the Institute of Tradition is still paying." She raised her flute to her pretend employer. "That's how Alicia and I met. I helped her out of a jam when I was on assignment in Greece. She's taken a shine to me ever since," she replied before taking another sip. The easiest lies to sell were the ones with a kernel of truth.

A spark flashed in his dark eyes as he recognized a kindred spirit. "God bless the whims of the wealthy or we'd both be out of a job," he remarked.

"I can think of worse ways to spend a Sunday," she agreed and quickly steered the conversation back to yesterday. "But I am sorry I arrived a day late. The way Alicia tells it, I missed the *absolute height* of drama and suspense." He grinned at her choice of words. He had a weak spot for tall women, and this one was clever and funny as well.

Martinez pitched him a softball question to establish she was an ignorant but enthusiastic audience. "Is it true none of the favorites took first?"

He nodded. "Never seen anything like it. Race after race."

"Something in the water? Or perhaps something shady?" she luridly suggested.

He shrugged his square shoulders. "Everyone's got a theory, especially on the races where they lost the most money, but I doubt it. The weather was fine, the track was neat, and they come down like hawks on even the suspicion of doping."

She lowered her voice. "But surely you knew your horse had a real shot of winning."

He leaned in until he was close enough to smell the almond and honey from her shampoo. "Between you, me, and this pillar, I didn't think Tall Boy had it in him. Don't get me wrong, he's a fine horse with a sweet temper—a real pleasure to ride—but among the field of competitors, with all the weight he was carrying?" He left the question unanswered but his facial expression spoke volumes.

"So when did you know you had it in the bag?" Her interest was genuine, albeit for reasons than Hennessy couldn't even begin to imagine.

He stared out as he replayed the race in his mind. "It was after the first turn. Something lit a fire under him and he was a different horse. It was like being on a runaway train. I would never have guessed that he could generate so much power.

While he was lost in memory, Martinez spooled out a thread of will with her words. "Do you remember hearing or seeing anything out of place?"

"No," he responded dreamily. "Just the relentless beat of hooves and the dust they kicked up."

She withdrew her magic with ease. "Sounds exhilarating." He blinked; her words returned him to the here and now.

He chose his phrasing carefully. "No greater high than riding a winner across the finish line."

Martinez smirked at the mischievous glint in his eyes. *That's how you deliver a come on.*

# Chapter Eleven

Louisville, Kentucky, USA
3rd of May, 12:25 p.m. (GMT-4)

Thoroughbreds have continuously raced at Churchill Downs since 1875, and all the horses had to be stabled somewhere, preferably away from the grandstand. Not everyone had a fondness for the smell of hay, manure, and oiled leather. Like other aspects of the complex, the stables had undergone a series of renovations over the years but were still quaintly referred to as the backside barns.

The distance seemed trivial from the panoramic windows at brunch but traversing the uneven ground in fashionable footwear was another matter. Fortunately, the weather was pleasant and Ian McGonagall walked at a leisurely pace to accommodate his two guests.

"How long have you been training horses?" Moncrief made conversation.

"Over thirty years, probably before either of you were born," he replied in good humor. "Started out in general training as a lad and was immediately hooked."

"What's the difference between general training and what

you do now?' Martinez asked from his other side.

McGonagall grinned at his good fortune. His horse had won, he had a full belly and a slight buzz, the weather was sunny and cool, and he had a lovely woman on either side of him who both wanted to hear about his work.

"General training is where horses get used to being handled and taking verbal cues from people. You also have to gradually introduce pressure around their middle before going full tack and then adding the weight of a rider. The idea is to get them used to these things at a young age so the trainer can focus on getting them race-ready, which is what I do now," he explained.

"How young?" Martinez inquired.

"Usually after the first year. I didn't start training Tall Boy for racing until he was almost two years old, which is fine. If you start intense training too young, you risk joint injury," he added sagely.

"How long has he been racing?" Moncrief took the baton.

"This is his fourth season, and probably his last," he responded with a little sadness. "There isn't a maximum age limit but most horses don't race after their sixth birthday. There's only so much experience can counter younger mature horses at their peak power."

"But horses live so much longer than that," Martinez objected. "What will happen to Tall Boy?"

"Don't worry, he's not going to the glue factory," he reassured her. "He'll finish the season and go to stud. He has respectable racing stats, especially with this win late in his career."

"Better to leave on a high note?" Martinez guessed.

"That and before he sustains a major injury that requires euthanasia," he said ominously as they approached the barns.

"And what will you do after Tall Boy retires?" Moncrief made small talk while Martinez took everything in, including the security cameras in the area. Even if she had the desire to salt cast the entire place, it would be a logistical nightmare. The most recent expansion increased the carrying capacity to 1,400 stalls with an adjacent quarantine facility and equine medical center.

"There's always work for an experienced trainer, but I'll miss Tall Boy. He's a good horse. Loves to run and takes well to training." Something in the way he said it made the ladies think that was the height of compliment. He patted down his pockets until he found his lanyard as they approached a manned choke point with full camera coverage. The guard gave the trio entry after a close inspection.

"This way," McGonagall directed them through the maze of stalls. There was a scattering of people among the stalls, even at lunch time on Sunday. The ones affiliated with a horse wore lanyards like McGonagall's and Churchill Downs staff had employee badges clipped to their coveralls.

"Hey, boy," the trainer called out before they actually reached Tall Boy's stall. He neighed at the familiar voice. The trainer motioned for the ladies to stand back until he made introductions.

McGonagall pulled out a sugar cube from his pocket, purloined from coffee service at brunch. "I brought you a treat and some guests, if you feel up to it," he prefaced before holding out his hand. "You gonna play nice?"

A reddish-brown horse head with tan spots and black tipped ears poked out of the stall. The bay thoroughbred snatched the sugar cube in his mouth and tilted his head. McGonagall reached up and gave him a good scratch behind the ears before patting his shoulder. Tall Boy nickered and the trainer stepped aside. "You can come close now. He's ready for visitors."

"He's so big," Martinez marveled. He was seventeen hands high and nearly a thousand pounds of lean muscle. She knew she must have seen horses in real life before, but none made quite the same impression as Tall Boy. While she was acutely aware of the animal's power, Moncrief was more taken by his appearance.

"He's gorgeous!" she softly exclaimed. No stranger to horses, she stepped forward and to the side, letting him see and smell her. Tall Boy batted his long eyelashes at her praise and allowed her to give his neck a smooth, firm stroke. He lowered his head and leaned into the petting.

"I think he likes you," McGonagall mused. "It's okay, Tracy, he's in a sociable mood. Just approach from the front and give him plenty of warning that you are coming close."

Martinez put her hand out and spoke sweetly like she

would with a dog. "Hey buddy. Aren't you a majestic horse?" Tall Boy saw her palm and lowered his head further.

"Oh, he's got an itch. Just put your palm flat between his eyes and give it a good firm rub," the Irishman coached her. Martinez followed his instructions to the letter and giggled as the horse whinnied in delight.

McGonagall took off his sports jacket and hung it up on a nearby hook. He unbuttoned his cuffs and started rolling them up. "Okay, boy. You've had a treat and a little love from the ladies. Time for business."

He crouched down and took off the dressing on Tall Boy's chest. Moncrief and Martinez looked over his shoulder and caught sight of the abrasion: a cross set in a square, not unlike a squat kite.

"How on earth did that happen?" Moncrief asked, bewildered. There was no tack on that part of the horse's chest.

"Haven't a clue. Found it after the race during grooming," McGonagall said as he cleaned the wound and examined it, "but it looks better than yesterday, which is the important thing." He put on gloves and applied a thin layer of petroleum jelly with antibiotics mixed in.

Tall Boy snorted low and McGonagall answered in a singsong voice. "I know, boy. You're doing great. I'll be done in a second." He pulled a new dressing and cloth tape from his field bag, only to find just one inch left at the end of the roll.

"Shite," he cursed under his breath. "I don't suppose

either of you keep paper or cloth tape in your purses?" They shook their heads in unison and sensed an opportunity on the horizon.

"They should have some in the medical center," he said, taking off his gloves.

"Is it all right if we stay?" Martinez asked, motioning to her heels.

"Sure," he said jovially. "Pull up a stool and keep Tall Boy company. I won't be but a few minutes."

As soon as the coast was clear, Moncrief pulled out her phone and took a picture of the wound while Martinez fished her vape pen out of her purse. She twisted the tip until the notches lined up, turning it into a saltcaster. With a forceful blow, white grains danced across the front of the stall. Tall Boy edged away from the magically imbued salt.

"It's okay, boy. We're friends," Moncrief cooed as Martinez kept watch, waiting for a pattern to emerge in her peripheral vision. Anyone viewing the security feed would see two women with sore feet taking a load off, one fiddling with her phone and the other vaping.

Martinez gave it a full minute while Moncrief continued talking to Tall Boy in dulcet tones, but the salt remained still in an even distribution. "Huh," Martinez grunted under her breath and knocked a sack over with her foot, giving her an excuse to grab a nearby broom and sweep the area.

Moncrief murmured without looking up, "I would have bet

my frosted pink Ferragamo slingbacks that mark was arcane."

Once the magic was dispersed from the salt, Tall Boy sniffed and tested it with his tongue. When he found it mundane, he lost interest in it and stepped forward, nudging his nose toward McGonagall's jacket that still hung beside his stall.

Moncrief rose and fished another sugar cube from the pocket. "Just one. I don't want to get in trouble with your trainer." The horse snorted, this time higher in his register.

"Can we stop by the track after this?" Martinez spoke out loud. "I'd like to see where the horses actually raced."

Moncrief read between the lines and bobbed her head. "I don't see why not." She offered the sugar cube to the thoroughbred and spoke quietly in his ear. Even though he couldn't understand the words, she believed the horse could pick up her intent. "We'll find out who did this to you, sweetie." She patted him on the shoulder twice. His long tongue licked her palm and his lips a few times, checking for any sugar crystals he'd missed the first time.

When McGonagall returned, they thanked him for the chance to meet Tall Boy and made their excuses. Once they were out of the barns, there was noticeably less security. They followed the path the horses would have taken to the track. There wasn't any signage, and the entrance was so inconspicuous that one could easily walk right past it without a second thought. The only hint that it was something important was a closed gate with an empty seat for a guard.

With the racing done for the weekend, it was low priority from a security standpoint. Churchill Downs was more focused on safeguarding what was valuable, i.e., the horses, and keeping the riffraff from cruising the luxury suites and millionaires' row. They didn't even give tours between the Thursday before and the Tuesday after Derby, which meant Martinez and Moncrief had the run of the place as long as they weren't stopped.

There were some cameras along the way, but they pressed on undeterred. On the surface, they were a pair of well-dressed upper-class women wandering around Churchill Downs. Anyone who recognized Moncrief would know she had a standing spot in the Mansion, the most exclusive seats that could only be purchased by invitation. Still, they didn't waste time and went straight to the first turn. Hennessy said that was where Tall Boy picked up the pace and that was where Martinez wanted to cast salt.

As soon as the white grains hit the ground, they started shifting, which immediately grabbed the agents' attention. The dispersed salt morphed into a magical signature and they both stood dumbfounded for a second before Moncrief snapped a picture.

"I'm new to reading these things," Martinez prefaced, "but that looks a whole lot like the signature of a fiend."

"Yup," Moncrief definitively dashed any hopes Martinez had that she was wrong in her interpretation. Her thumbs were moving double time as she submitted the picture to the Mine.

"Demon, if I had to guess, but Chloe and Dot will know for sure."

Martinez calmly put forth the question they were both thinking. "How the hell did no one notice a demon in the middle of the Kentucky Derby?"

"No idea," Moncrief admitted. "But I think it's time to divide and conquer."

# Chapter Twelve

Louisville, Kentucky, USA
3rd of May, 2:06 p.m. (GMT-4)

Tyler Green didn't mind going to church on Sunday. Each week, he showed up in a suit and tie and gave his tithe without complaint or being showy about it. He generally liked the music, and the praise songs were growing on him although there hadn't been any percussion or guitars at church when he was growing up except at the hippy church on the other side of town.

The pastor kept his sermons short, sweet, and to the point, especially on game days. There were always refreshments, even if he had to endure the same joke week after week about how cops couldn't resist free coffee and donuts. There was nothing wrong with fellowship on Sunday, but some people didn't know when to leave well enough alone.

It started out small: an egg hunt on Easter, vacation bible study during the summer, a fall festival to give the children a safe alternative to Halloween, and a Christmas pageant. Special events led to regular obligations: prayer meetings midweek, women's bible study on Fridays, men's bible study on Tuesdays, youth group for the kids on Saturday. Then it seeped into secular life: buying group tickets to amusement parks, going on vacation with other families from church, and last year they ate Valentine's dinner in the redecorated gym, served by the youth group. That was how he came to be at a potluck with no beer or booze: someone had the bright idea of having a wholesome—read: dry—Derby party after service.

For the most part, he kept his annoyance to himself for his family's sake. An active church life allowed them to have a structured social life and things to look forward to despite the irregular schedule that work sometimes demanded of him. There was worse company for them to keep while he was on duty, so he kept his mouth shut and helped himself to another country ham sandwich. He washed it down with a mint mocktail while his kids played and his wife socialized on behalf of them both.

He was a little ashamed that relief was his first instinct when his phone rang, but he really couldn't care less about Kyle's new riding mower or what Maggie read about avocados on the internet. He excused himself and moved away for some privacy.

There were raised eyebrows, but everyone knew better than to ask what was going on. Tyler Green was as tight-lipped as they came, especially when it came to official police business. His wife kept the conversation going but also kept tabs on his call—she didn't just have eyes on the back of her head but could split her hearing as well.

"Hello," he answered. He knew the precinct was calling, even if the caller ID hadn't told him as much. Anyone else he knew would have messaged him.

"Sorry to interrupt your Sunday, Sarge, but we've got a situation and I thought I should let you know," the voice on the other line started apologetically. Green recognized its owner as one of his detectives.

"Bad news isn't going to smell better with time," he replied.

"We got a call from a neighbor about activity inside last night's dog mauling in Parkland. Dispatch sent a couple of uniforms over, and they encountered a woman claiming she was from the FBI. She presented her ID and had a search warrant on her, but they phoned it in anyway."

Green heard what wasn't being said and asked, "Who did they send?"

"Johnson and MacIntyre," the man on the line replied.

"Christ," Green cursed before he remembered where he was and silently apologized to God. "Anyone hurt?"

"Just Johnson's pride when she got the jump on him." The junior detective didn't bother to conceal his schadenfreude. Johnson's ego could stand to take a few hits and the fact that it was a woman from the FBI was just gravy.

"Well, no harm there," Green said lightly. "Tell the boys to stand down and let her do her work. I'll head there and smooth everything over. What's this FBI agent's name?"

There was an audible shuffle of papers before he answered. "Special Agent Teresa Martinez."

"Got it. I'm still at church and I want to leave the car for Katie. Send a squad car to come get me—First Baptist on Jefferson," Green directed his subordinate.

"Will do, Sarge."

His wife came over as soon as he hung up. She could tell from his expression that he was leaving, but she wanted to know how serious it was. Whenever something gruesome happened, he preferred to have his family safe at home, even if they weren't personally at risk.

"Do we need to go?" she asked simply.

He smiled at the offer but shook his head. "No, you and kids stay and enjoy yourselves. You got your keys?"

"In my purse," she answered and automatically dug them out as proof. She knew the drill by now.

He gave his standard proviso, "I shouldn't be late, but I'll call if it ends up that way." His eyes darkened as his mind shifted from church social to police work.

Katie squeezed his upper arm to stop him from drifting away just yet. He looked down and found her expression serious despite her loving gaze. "Be careful."

"Always," he promised and planted a kiss on her cheek. She nodded and returned to the others while he made his way to the front of the church with a quizzical look on his face. *What interest does the FBI have in a dog mauling?*

Martinez watched the squad car drive away before she resumed her search. She had already salt cast and searched the living room and kitchen before she was rudely interrupted. When it came to looking for magic, she always started at the points of violence.

The single-story house didn't have a basement and the attic was little more than a crawl space packed with pink insulation, so she turned her attention to the bathrooms and bedrooms. Her diligence was rewarded when she found the duffle bag filled with bricks of cash stashed deep in one of the closets. She emptied the bag and checked the seams for hidden pockets, but it was what it was: a pile of money. She counted each stack as she put it back in the canvas: just shy of ten thousand. It wasn't his winnings, as they were still being transferred from his gambling account to his bank account. She bagged and tagged it, going through the motions of collecting evidence like a normal FBI agent.

She'd captured a magical signature in the kitchen—this one decidedly not fiendish—but found no arcane or occult supplies. It struck her as odd because summoners usually secured a dedicated ritual space with all their necessary kit so they wouldn't be interrupted mid-summoning. Those that summoned fast and loose didn't have a long life expectancy because the smallest slip-up could spell disaster. Martinez thought it unlikely that Kinkade used the kitchen for such endeavors and had the Mine digging for storage rentals and other properties while the second floor worked on the magical signature from the kitchen. Mark Kinkade wasn't registered as a practitioner, but that didn't mean he wasn't in the system.

Once she hit the morgue, she would know definitively if he was a magician and the owner of the signature in the kitchen. If he ticked all the boxes, his death was likely a swift karmic backlash and there wouldn't be anything left to do but find where he'd summoned the demon and get rid of any dangerous material. *But when is it ever that simple?* the cynical part of her piped up.

She couldn't prove it yet, but her instincts told her Kinkade was involved. She returned to the living room. On first pass, something about the scene hadn't sat right with her, but she'd forced herself to set that aside until she had finished her search for evidence of arcane activity. It was no longer her job to investigate deaths unless magic was involved, but it was hard to turn off her investigative instinct.

The one upside of running into Tweedledee and Tweedledum was getting more information about Mark Kinkade's death from them. According to the officers, he was found in the recliner with his throat ripped out and a knife in hand while his dog was found dead in the kitchen. They reasoned that Kinkade grabbed the knife and cut the dog before he died, and the dog retreated to the kitchen and bled out from his wounds. They had called it an open and shut case, but it was a little too convenient for her and the gnawing feeling in her gut definitely wasn't hunger.

She closed her eyes and cleared her mind. It was an old trick she'd learned at the FBI—when what you see doesn't make sense, reset and look at it with new eyes. She opened her eyes and scanned the room through a mundane lens: a battered recliner soaked in blood with splatter on the nearby furniture, dried crimson paw prints on the worn carpet, and a swinging door to the kitchen. There wasn't any blood splatter that far out from the recliner, but there were low smudges, presumably made by the dog in retreat.

With her gloved hand, she pushed the connecting door open and entered the kitchen. She gave the bloodstain on the linoleum a wide berth and took a global view of the room. The stream of blood splatter on the kitchen side of the door stuck out like a sore thumb. *If Kinkade had his throat ripped out in the living and he wounded the dog before he died, then why is there blood spatter on this side of the door?*

She looked for dark red specks on any nearby surface in case the dog was covered in blood and shook himself after the attack. The peeling wallpaper, the scratched Formica countertop, the thick wooden kitchen table, and the dated cabinets and fixtures were all free of blood. Then she opened the door again, this time from the other side. If the dog had been stabbed in the kitchen and chased Kinkade into the living room, there should have been arterial spray along the entire path, not just by the recliner.

"Then whose blood is on the kitchen door?" Martinez wondered out loud. Someone or something was attacked in the kitchen and the cops' version of events didn't account for it. She checked the back door, and the subtle signs of forced entry confirmed her suspicions—there had been another person here.

Her mind immediately flooded with possibilities and questions. *Did Kinkade have a partner that turned on him? Was he hired help that became a loose end and had to be dealt with once the Derby was over? How does the dog fit in all this?*

A loud knock on the front door pulled her out of her contemplation and a second later she heard her name. "Special Agent Martinez? Are you in there?"

"In the kitchen," she called out and summoned her will in case the company was less than welcoming. *Hail Mary, full of grace…*

She quickly sized up what came through the door: a man of average build, five feet ten, 170-190 lbs., brown hair, brown eyes, dressed in a nondescript blue suit and generic blue and red striped tie. The fine lines around his eyes deepened as he smiled and extended his hand. "I'm Sergeant Tyler Green of the Louisville Police Department," he introduced himself.

Martinez gave him a firm shake and released her will. "You

boys sure know how to roll out the welcome mat. Should I expect the chief of police next?" she drily joked.

He chuckled politely at her comment and took a conciliatory tone. "I don't see any reason to take this higher up. I'm just here to apologize for my overzealous officers and see if there is anything we can do to help further your investigation."

Martinez had been in bureaucracy long enough to recognize damage control. She tested the waters. "A chance to review any photos of the scene taken when they found the body would be helpful. And any personal items collected."

Green nodded thoughtfully; she was willing to play ball and negotiations had begun. "I don't see a problem there. All that should be at the station."

"And expedited access to the body of the deceased and the dog would help me wrap things up faster," she added. LaSalle had prepared the necessary paperwork for her to get access to Kinkade's body, but death-by-dog was an unexpected development.

"That's not exactly my purview, but I'll make a few calls," he agreed. "But surely this was an unfortunate happenstance. A man's dog attacked him and he mortally wounded it in self-defense, but not before it ripped out his throat. Nothing to investigate there except to rule out rabies."

Martinez made direct eye contact and gave the same spiel she gave local law enforcement time and time again. "The deceased is a person of interest in an ongoing investigation. Therefore, his death is also of interest, regardless the circumstances."

"Fair enough," Green conceded, recognizing an official stonewall when he heard it. "If you're ready, I can get you set up at the station with what we have and see what I can do about the bodies. I know the dog will be examined and tested, but it's up to the ME to decide whether Mr. Kinkade's body requires an autopsy," he informed her before slyly adding, "unless he is given a reason to question the nature of his death."

Martinez played it cool. "It's still his corpse so it's his call, but I would like to see the body, even if a full autopsy isn't conducted."

# Chapter Thirteen

Marilyn Wilkes slipped into the administration building and took the back way to her office. She still had her phone on in case there was an honest emergency, but she screened her calls and messages judiciously. Everyone thought their concern constituted an emergency. All the horses may have crossed the finish line, but her Derby wasn't over until Churchill Downs returned to normal operations.

The desks were empty and the overhead fluorescents off. Everyone working that day was catering to either the guests or the animals. Once she was safely behind her locked office door, the stylish brunette slipped out of her heels and gave her dimples a rest. Like any hostess at the end of a long visit, she was ready to send the visitors packing.

She didn't bother switching on the lights. She craved a measure of peace and quiet after performing a nonstop string of professional and social duties. Plus, lights would only give away her location, and Wilkes didn't want to be found, at least not for a little while.

From the bottom drawer of her desk, she pulled out a bottle of amber liquor and a glass—it was not Woodford Reserve and therefore had to be kept out of plain sight. As media coordinator, optics were everything. The sweet woody notes flooded her nostrils as soon as she took off the top. She poured herself a generous three fingers and sipped her neat bourbon out of her Waterford tumbler in the silent darkness. It was absolute bliss.

The actual staging of the Derby went smoothly. There was the typical array of complications and kerfuffles, but nothing disastrous. The media coverage was a rousing success; all things Derby were still trending, especially #CinderellaDerby.

However, you can't please all the people all the time. For every happy winner, there was a litter of losers. While most took it on the chin, there was always a vocal minority. This year, it was the magicians by a mile. Each year, they cooked up elaborate schemes to cheat the system and then cried foul when they didn't win. Unfortunately for Wilkes, she wasn't just the media coordinator. She was also in charge of magical security.

A soft knock fell on the door and Wilkes froze. She hoped whoever it was would go away if she didn't make a sound or move a muscle. "I know you're in there, Lynn," a high-pitched voice sharply cut through the solid door. Then it sweetened. "I have dessert and champagne, and not the swill they use in the mimosas," it called to her like a siren.

Wilkes relaxed as soon as she identified the speaker and rose to unlock the door. "Quick, before anyone sees you," she shooed the petite form of Alicia Moncrief. The heiress darted inside and put her offerings on the desk while Wilkes secured the door. "How did you know I would be in here?"

"Woman's intuition," she answered coyly. The brunette gave her a hard stare. "And your PA gave me a hint."

"Jenny and I are going to have to a talk," Wilkes said darkly as Moncrief unwrapped the top.

"Don't be too hard on her," Moncrief came to her defense as she popped open the bottle. Wilkes grabbed the flutes and caught the bubbly. "I had to turn the screws pretty far before I got it out of her, and who can resist me for very long?" When Moncrief set down the bottle, she spied the brandy. "That bad?"

"And only 364 days until the next Derby!" Wilkes exclaimed sarcastically. Moncrief giggled and it was infectious. Wilkes softened at the sight of her effervescent friend and it wasn't long until she was genuinely smiling. She handed Moncrief a full glass and they clinked the crystal before taking a sip.

"Well, this year was brilliant," Moncrief said emphatically as she grabbed the platter of bourbon balls. She took a seat in one of the oversized chairs and left the sofa for Wilkes. "I missed the Oaks, but yesterday was one of the more exciting days of racing I've attended. And the spread was killer."

"Isn't the new chef great?" Wilkes agreed. "I sniped him from a three-star Michelin restaurant," she said proudly as she followed the chocolate covered treats. "Don't let my dour mood fool you, Ali—I'm thrilled to bits. Viewership and consumer engagement are up, the sponsors are happy, and I've already got companies asking about advertising for next year." She stretched her legs along the length of the sofa and popped a bourbon ball into her mouth.

Moncrief tilted her head theatrically. "Then why so serious?"

"Oh, you know…rich practitioners are the *worst* losers," she declared with exasperation. Moncrief nodded because she knew it was true. "Not to name names, but one owner was so incensed that they failed to see the irony in their complaint." Wilkes screwed her face into a scowl, lowered her register, and filled it with bluster. "How could my horse have lost when I tried so hard to rig the race in my favor?!"

Moncrief guffawed. "You're kidding?!"

Wilkes laughed despite how tired she was. "Not in so many words, but you get the gist."

"But you're not worried," Moncrief surmised.

The brunette in repose shook her head. "They'll be out of my hair in two days."

"Because there's talk," Moncrief stated simply.

"Ali, there's always talk," Wilkes countered.

"True, but there's a lot of chatter this year, enough for *me* to take note. It could mean trouble, Lynn," Moncrief argued. "There are still a fair number of people who weren't happy about you getting the position."

"The usual masculine disillusionment in discovering that a woman has a brain," she quoted one of her favorite authors. "I appreciate the concern, but the adjudicators know the magical security here is sound. They'll hear the complaints as a formality, and we'll all move on."

"And what if they found something?" Moncrief asked in a tone that was both light and loaded.

Wilkes sat up. "You know something." It wasn't a question but a statement of fact.

"Nothing I can elaborate on, but I would like to help," the blonde answered truthfully without saying too much.

Wilkes sighed. "And you know I can't talk about the kind of security in place."

Moncrief fiddled with her hair while she brainstormed, a bad habit supposedly eradicated in finishing school but it still cropped up occasionally. Clearly, they were both bound by oaths, but there had to be a way for them to help each other without breaking them.

Wilkes knew Moncrief had cooked up a scheme when her blue eyes gleamed and her smile took on a wicked disposition in spite of her dimples. She was well acquainted with Moncrief's mischievous streak.

Moncrief released her locks and smoothed her skirt before settling her hands in her lap. "What if I put forth possible scenarios, and you tell me if they are possible with the current security measures in place?" she proposed. She helped herself to a bourbon ball and let her friend think it over.

Wilkes bit her lip as she entertained the notion. If it were anyone else, it would have been an automatic no...but this was

Ali. She was one of the few people from school that Wilkes actually liked and historically, she had always had her back. She wouldn't even have this job if Moncrief hadn't vouched for her magical ability and integrity. "Okay, counselor, I'll allow it, but proceed with caution."

Moncrief started with an easy question to test her workaround. "Could someone bring something enchanted into the race?"

"Yes, but it wouldn't work during the race," Wilkes replied with ease. It was a no brainer and something that everyone knew, but the fact that she was able to answer the question was illuminating.

"How about someone on the sidelines or in the stands? Could they use magic to affect what's happening on the track?" she asked.

"Not once the race starts," Wilkes responded truthfully without hesitation.

"Could someone cast a spell or perform a ritual beforehand and have it remain in effect during a race?" Moncrief spitballed.

Wilkes shook her head. "Not without being part of our wards."

"Could someone participating in the race cast a spell while on the track?" she inquired, hoping to narrow the field of arcane possibilities.

Wilkes's perfectly sculpted right eyebrow raised. "While they're steering a thousand pounds of muscle running at top speed?" she asked dubiously.

"For the sake of argument," Moncrief encouraged her to answer.

"Kudos to anyone who could get a spell off in those conditions, but it wouldn't matter," she said dismissively. "I would know about it and then they would be at the mercy of the adjudicators."

"And you don't know of any casting that took place on the track yesterday?" Moncrief followed up for completeness.

Wilkes rolled her eyes. "Obviously not, Ali, or we wouldn't be having this conversation." Moncrief smirked at her blunt honesty peppered with sarcasm. Everyone needed someone in their lives to tell them when they were being a dumbass, and she never had to worry about Lynn sugarcoating the truth. It was easy for someone in her position to become comfortable in an echo chamber of sycophants, which made people like Lynn worth their weight in gold.

"Hypothetically, if someone in the race did cast a spell and got it off, could it work?" Moncrief pressed forward.

Wilkes became quiet. "Possibly," she reluctantly conceded a weak spot in the security. As soon as she uttered the last syllable, she felt a niggling in the back of her mind that grew into a full squirm. The keeper of the wards was treading close to dangerous ground. "But I can't say what would or wouldn't work, so don't ask," she quickly warned Moncrief.

The blonde nodded and continued her quest to figure out

how the fiendish signature got on the track. She'd wanted to ask about summoning but had to approach it from a different direction. "What about supernatural creatures...could they be present on the track during a race?"

Wilkes ran through all the variables that would have to line up to pull it off. "Theoretically, but it's highly unlikely."

"Because they would have to be summoned during a race but after it had already started?" she guessed.

Wilkes was unable to answer, and Moncrief took her silence as confirmation. "Don't worry, Lynn. You don't have to say anything more," she reassured her friend and gave her a bright smile.

"Have another bourbon ball. Your pâtissier has outdone themselves," she gaily changed the subject. "Did you see what Gertrude Windom was wearing yesterday?" Moncrief watched the tension in Wilkes's body dissipate as she changed to lighter topics.

Wilkes reached over and grabbed another chocolate-covered confection, one topped with plenty of pecans. "I don't think anyone could miss it. I'm pretty sure it had its own hashtag at one point."

# Chapter Fourteen

Martinez parked her rental car next to the dirty Range Rover in the otherwise empty parking lot, pleased with the direction the day had taken. What had started out as an annoying run-in with Louisville PD had become a productive afternoon. She had copies of the photos taken last night as well as statements from the neighbors and the deceased's friend that had found the body and called 911. After going through Kinkade's personal possessions, she had taken his cell phone and the bag of ash that was in his pocket as evidence. Ash was a known arcane component and if it had been used ritualistically, the sixth floor may be able to pull information from it using the esoteric version of mass spectrometry. The locals had assumed it was for drug testing and she didn't correct them.

Sergeant Green wasn't able to coax the medical examiner off the golf course, but he was able to get him on the phone. The ME had cleaned and examined the body that morning and confirmed the cause of death was exsanguination secondary to animal bite. He'd hastily agreed to send her a copy of his report when it was finished before she lost him to the eleventh hole.

At the morgue, she had to use a little of her will to get a moment alone with the corpse. There was no magical signature upon salt casting; Kinkade was not a practitioner nor had he been killed by magic. Martinez's best guess was that Kinkade was in cahoots with a practitioner because he'd had access to the horses by virtue of being a Churchill Downs employee, which would explain why he had ash on his person when he died. If this practitioner had an aptitude with enchanting horses, it was also possible that the dog wasn't acting under its own accord when it killed its owner. But there was only one way to find out.

She locked the car and approached the gray building labeled Department of Animal Control. The door was open despite the "closed" sign hanging in the window. When she entered, an electronic bell chimed but there was no one at the counter to greet her and the lights were off.

"Hello? Is anyone here?" she called out into the dark, empty room. *This is how horror movies start*, she thought to herself as she waited for a response.

"In the back," she heard a voice holler.

Martinez took that as an invitation and ventured deeper into the building. She passed by a door and the caged animals behind it made a huge ruckus. She knew it was more than just dogs, but she couldn't pick out the different species in the cacophony. "Don't mind them," the same voice yelled. "They've been squirrelly all afternoon."

She followed the folksy twang into a room further down the hall. Inside, a woman with protective gear over her jeans and a t-shirt was standing over a dissected corpse. "Dr. Cassandra Schultz?" Martinez inquired.

The woman discreetly pulled a sheet over the body before looking up. Her curly brown hair was pulled back away from her face, which was tanned and au natural. Martinez pegged her somewhere in her early fifties. "Call me Cassie. And you must be the woman from the FBI that's got Ty by the balls," she said humorously.

Martinez grinned and introduced herself. "I'm Special Agent Martinez. I appreciate you coming in on a Sunday." She declined to extend her hand as the vet's gloved hands were covered in bodily fluids.

Schultz was a woman who knew her own mind, and it didn't take long for the vet to size up her visitor from behind her safety goggles. "Well, it's not every day the FBI wants to know about an animal death, and I'm getting a bottle of single malt that's old enough to vote out of it." Schultz's disposition was still surly but no longer directed at Martinez, which she took as a sign that she passed muster. "You got a queasy stomach, Special Agent Martinez?"

"No ma'am," she answered respectfully and grabbed a pair of gloves from the box on the counter. Schultz pulled back the sheet and watched Martinez to see if she was true to her word;

she approved when the agent didn't so much as flinch.

Martinez was no stranger to dead bodies, but it was her first time visiting a veterinarian doing a postmortem on a dog. Comparative anatomy wasn't a hobby of hers and it had been many years since she'd dissected animals in biology class. "This is my first animal autopsy," she admitted as she looked over the gory mass in front of her. "What am I looking at?"

"This is the remains of Baxter Kinkade. Because he was implicated in the death of a human, I am performing a necropsy. Autopsies are for people, necropsies are for animals," Schultz educated her. "Basically, I'm looking for why a normally sweet dog attacked his owner."

Martinez picked up on her familiarity. "You knew Baxter?"

"He was one of my patients," she replied. "Per protocol, I'll send tissue samples from the brain for testing, but I'll tell you right now, it's not rabies. Baxter was up-to-date on his vaccinations."

"Could it have been abuse?" Martinez suggested.

Schultz's body language indicated that she categorically rejected the idea, but she answered like she'd entertained the notion. "Anything's possible but I doubt it. His owner was good about bringing him in for regular checkups and vaccinations, and Baxter never displayed signs of abuse." Martinez was amused that the vet used the dog's name liberally but Mark Kinkade was simply "his owner."

"What exactly do you look for in a necropsy?" Martinez

deliberately used the correct jargon.

Schultz picked up a surgical tool and talked while she cut, "Organic causes for abrupt behavioral changes—things like illnesses causing end-organ damage, brain tumors, other neurologic changes—"

"Any luck?"

"Not yet," the vet answered as precisely as she sliced at the connective tissue, careful not to damage the underlying organs.

"Do you know how Baxter died?"

"Laceration across the throat," she answered immediately. "Based on the damage to the tissue, a serrated edge in a single decisive movement."

Martinez's brow furrowed. "In your expert opinion, could Baxter have gone very far after sustaining such an injury?"

Schultz shook her head back and forth. "I wouldn't think so. It was pretty deep. It severed the carotid artery and the windpipe, and death would have been almost instantaneous. I suppose he could have taken a few steps. Why do you ask?"

"I'm just trying to recreate what happened last night since neither Baxter nor his owner will be able to tell us," Martinez mimicked the vet's predilections. "The police found a bread knife at the scene and it was the only knife missing from the butcher block," she elaborated to draw attention away from the fact that Mark Kinkade could not have killed his dog.

"Bread knife fits the bill," Schultz agreed.

"In your preliminary observations, did anything strike you

as odd or out of place?" Martinez asked broadly.

"It's funny you ask, but there's a mark on the skin just on the back of the neck that I don't remember being there before." Schultz set the scalpel down and used both hands to maneuver the body into a different angle. "If it were any other shape, I would chalk it up to ringworm."

Martinez combed the newly exposed fur with her gloved fingers, separated the matted bloody hair until she could see it clearly—a line with a bent tip on one end and a half circle on the other.

"That is strange. Mind if I take a picture?" Martinez asked as she fished her phone out of her pocket with her clean hand.

"Suit yourself," the vet replied.

She ran her fingers over it. It was raised but also pigmented. "It almost looks like a fresh tattoo," she observed. "It that something people do to dogs?"

"Sure, we do it in our practice for owners who don't want to chip," Schultz replied as she laid the body back down on the table. "But I don't think that's what this is. For starters, tattooed identifiers are usually a combination of letters and numbers, not a symbol. And it wouldn't be on the scruff of the neck. We usually put ours on the belly or the inside of the hind legs where the hair is kept short. Plus, Baxter had a chip."

*Hail Mary, full of grace…* Martinez summoned her will and created a crash everyone could hear emanating from the room where the live animals were stored. All hell broke loose once the dogs started barking.

"What are you troublemakers up to now?" Schultz shouted. She covered Baxter's partially dissected body with a sheet before taking off her dirty gloves. "Excuse me, I have to check on the animals," she apologized.

Martinez nodded sympathetically. "Baxter and I will be here when you get back."

As soon as the vet exited the exam room, Martinez quickly pulled out her vape pen and cast salt over the sheet. It wouldn't take Schultz long to find nothing was wrong, but Martinez only needed a minute. She pulled out her phone and set it to camera mode while she waited. The salt started to shake and dance, moving along the sheet without regard to the underlying contours or the basic laws of physics. It was the same magical signature in Kinkade's kitchen, and all the proof Martinez needed to absolve Baxter of his death.

She took a picture as soon as the pattern set and snapped the sheet with a flick of the wrists to disperse the magic and the salt. She lifted a corner and pulled a few hairs from near the tattoo. Then she turned her gloves inside out as she took them off, trapping the fur inside. She put her phone, vape pen, and waded gloves away and was washing her hands at the sink when a befuddled Schultz reentered the room.

"You heard that crashing sound too, right?"

"Yeah," Martinez affirmed as she dried her hands. "Did something fall over?"

"No, and everyone was still in their cages," the vet responded, puzzled.

Martinez casually shrugged. "Huh, that's weird. It must have been something outside."

# Chapter Fifteen

Louisville, Kentucky, USA
3rd of May, 5:38 p.m. (GMT-4)

Despite the hotel staff's best efforts, Martinez carted everything to the suite herself, although she did accept a luggage cart. In her mind, this was evidence, and even though no one would yell at her for breaking the chain of evidence, it was the principle of the matter. When she opened the door, she found Moncrief at the writing desk, eyes glued to her laptop.

The blonde pulled her attention away from the screen and smiled at the haul Martinez wheeled into the living area. "You've been productive."

She closed the door behind her and slipped off her jacket and shoes. "I still don't know who's summoning demons, but it's a start. How about you?"

"I wasn't able to get specifics on the magical security, but essentially, the wards on the track nullify magic at the start of each race and it's a closed system until the race is over," Moncrief summed up her thoughts.

"Someone on the track during the race?" Martinez took a stab as she rubbed her feet. Her boots were more comfortable than her heels, but the walk around Churchill Downs earlier had left its mark.

Moncrief frowned and shook her head. "Even if someone managed to summon a demon in under two minutes without a summoning circle, there's some sort of magical alarm if someone casts on the track during a race. My source says no alarms were triggered yesterday. It's a conundrum—on paper, it couldn't have happened but here we are."

Martinez's mind went to the obviously question. "How reliable is your source?"

"Very. Even if someone lower down the food chain had been compromised, she's solid," the blonde said confidently.

"Someone could have tampered with the wards," Martinez brainstormed. "When's the last time they were checked?"

"She didn't say—magical security at the track is very hush-hush—but I suspect she'll take a closer look at it after our talk."

Martinez didn't welcome the possibility of a roving band of vigilante magicians muddying the waters of an investigation, but it seemed wasteful not to use Moncrief's connections.

"Hopefully, I've insinuated myself deep enough to get Wilson inside as my private security specialist once they figure out someone went wrong," Moncrief continued. "If anyone can figure out how this practitioner got around those wards, it's him."

"I don't know of anyone better at summoning or security," Martinez wholeheartedly agreed. "Any headway on what we got this morning?"

"Chloe and Dot confirmed the signature on the track as demonic. It didn't match anything, but they are pretty sure it's a blood demon."

"Don't all fiends like blood?" Martinez asked skeptically on her way to change out of her work clothes.

"Sure, but blood demons are fueled by it and derive power from it," Moncrief explained. "Also, I finished going over your pictures and video from brunch."

"Any hits?" she asked from the bathroom.

"I found four practitioners and sent screenshots to the Mine. I wasted a lot of time before I realized there was a waitress with a nice ass producing a lot of false positives, but I was able to cull the numbers down with the video you took," Moncrief wryly filled her in.

"Everyone looks, but the good ones don't get caught," Martinez joked as she meticulously hung her suit up. A long steamy shower should get the wrinkles out if she needed another wear. She emerged in jeans and a knit top. "I was thinking of staying in for dinner and getting a better look at all this, but don't let me keep you from any plans you may have already had."

Moncrief considered her options: room service in her pajamas or getting dolled up for dinner with her Aunt Bethany and whatever eligible bachelor she'd rustled up at the last minute. That woman wouldn't be happy until Moncrief was married with a litter of her own. "They have a serviceable burgoo here," she answered indirectly and tossed Martinez the room service menu.

She caught it in one hand and read the description out loud, "A hearty meat stew made with chicken, beef, and lamb simmered with garden-fresh vegetables, beans, and vine-ripened tomatoes. Served in a sourdough bread bowl with a side salad." Her stomach growled. "Sold."

Moncrief phoned room service and placed their order while Martinez pulled back her hair into a messy bun and unpacked the cart. Next, she called her aunt and made her excuses. Martinez only heard half the conversation, but it wasn't hard to fill in the blanks.

"Aunt Bethany? It's Alicia. I'm sorry to call on such short notice, but I'm not going to make it tonight." Her voice and facial expression oozed sincere regret. "A friend came in from out of town at the last minute, and we're making a night of it." Martinez snorted at the blatant lie but Moncrief didn't break character.

The outcry from the other side of the line was so loud, even Martinez could hear it. The words were unintelligible but the tone was unmistakable.

"No, it's not a man," Moncrief said dismissively. "Of course, I would tell you if I was seeing someone," she insisted.

"It's no one you know—a friend from one of my charitable organizations," she patiently continued after a brief pause.

"I don't think that's a good idea. She would be bored to tears and what kind of host would that make me?" Martinez smiled as Moncrief artfully turned the tables against her relation. She made worming out of a previous engagement look so effortless.

"I tell you what, why don't we plan for a luncheon during Preakness Stakes, just the ladies. Maybe high tea? Baltimore is lovely this time of year." Martinez could tell from the change in pitch that Aunt Bethany approved of this idea.

Moncrief nodded her head while her aunt rattled off names. "That sounds fine! You make up a guest list and give me a final head count, and I'll make the arrangements."

"I know, I'm disappointed too," she lamented theatrically, "but we had a grand time yesterday and we'll see each other soon."

"I will. Give my best to everyone and we'll talk soon."

Martinez held her applause until she put her phone down. Moncrief curtsied and bowed; she knew it was a grand performance and had no problem receiving praise for it. She looked at the clock on the wall. "Food shouldn't be too much longer. Wanna show me what you've got while we wait?"

Martinez had everything laid out systematically and Moncrief took a seat beside her. "This is Mark Kinkade. He died last night after he returned from a shift at Churchill Downs. His dog ripped out his throat in the living room, but the dog was found dead in the kitchen." Moncrief flipped through the pictures of the crime scene as Martinez spoke. "I've got his phone, but it's locked so I won't get much out of it until I get tech on it. However, he did have a pocket full of ash and I'm hoping either Weber or the twins can get some information from it."

Moncrief immediately recognized the significance of ash. "Is he our magician?"

"No. I think he was hired help because there was a duffle bag full of cash in his house. He had free reign in the barns as an employee and no one would question why he was there."

Moncrief nodded—no one paid attention to the staff. She worked out for herself what came next. "But once the Derby was over, he's no longer useful."

"Exactly. I think the magician broke in, charmed the dog into killing Kinkade, and then killed the dog and staged it to look like they killed each other." Martinez pulled up the gallery on the phone and picked the relevant photos. "I found this magical signature in his kitchen as well as on the dog's body."

Moncrief glanced at the phone and compared the two signatures. Despite the difference in angles and lighting, they did look the same. "That's low, using a man's dog to kill him."

"Right?!" Martinez uttered with disdain before continuing with her show and tell. "This is the mark that was on the back of the dog's neck. It's different than the one on Tall Boy, but I'm pretty sure it's arcane. I sent it to Chloe and Dot for identification."

Moncrief's brow furrowed as she took a good look at the

picture. She rotated its orientation with a swipe of her finger. "No need; I know what that is. That's a *was* stick, also known as the scepter of Anubis."

Martinez stared at her in disbelief. "Why do you know that?"

She shrugged her slim shoulders. "My maternal grandparents were obsessed with all things Egyptian. While other kids were making sandcastles on the beach, we were excavating a tomb. Incidentally, Anubis is the god of the underworld and had a canine head," she added thoughtfully.

"Well, I got a few of the hairs from near the mark just in case."

Moncrief grinned. "That's how I know Wilson trained you."

Martinez laughed. "Spend enough time with anyone and their crazy rubs off on you."

"So, our working theory is that a practitioner hires a Churchill Downs employee to mark the winners with ash. Something involving a blood demon happens on the track during the race that gets the horse fired up. And then said magician ties up loose ends by charming his accomplice's dog to kill its owner?" Moncrief strung together the narrative to see if it held water. "I've heard of crazier schemes, but there's one thing I don't get."

"Only one?" Martinez asked sarcastically.

"Why kill the dog?" the heiress wondered. "It's not like the dog can rat you out, and it would be put down the second the body was found anyway. Why go through the hassle of killing it and framing the dead guy with the knife?"

Martinez paused and thought it through. She'd focused so myopically on the individual clues that she'd lost sight of the bigger picture. "They wouldn't," she admitted reluctantly. "Unless..." The gnawing feeling in her gut returned.

Martinez grabbed the stack of pictures and shuffled through them until she found the one she was looking for. She couldn't believe she'd missed it the first time—the bloody paw prints went in both directions. She mentally rearranged the order of events and all became crystal clear.

"Unless?" Moncrief prompted her to share her thoughts.

"Unless the dog was killed before it attacked Kinkade," Martinez finished her sentence. She put the crime scene photos in the right order. "We know the dog tore out Kinkade's throat in the living room. We know the magician broke in and cast their voodoo in the kitchen. The arterial spray on the kitchen side of the connecting door suggests the dog was killed in the kitchen. But not *after* the dog killed his owner. Before."

She pointed to the picture of the living room carpet. "The only way there could be bloody paw prints coming from the kitchen into the living room is if there was already a pool of blood in the kitchen. That's why the knife had to be found in Kinkade's hand—the dog was already dead when it killed him."

Moncrief looked more closely at the photos and shook her

head ominously. "Which means best case, we are looking for a reanimator—"

"And worst case, a necromancer," Martinez finished her thought.

Metaphysically speaking, there were numerous points of distinction between the two. No doubt Chloe and Dot could write an entire dissertation on it, but the quick and dirty boiled down to this: animators brought inanimate objects to life, reanimators brought dead things back to life, and necromancers stuffed souls into dead bodies. The first two were powered by the magician's will, the latter by a living soul that was esoterically caged inside a decaying vessel.

"God, I hate necromancers," Moncrief uttered with contempt. "Either way, we're going to have to burn the dog's body—the sooner, the better."

Scenes from *Pet Cemetery* flashed through Martinez's mind. She reached for her phone and started typing. "LaSalle shouldn't have any problems getting paperwork for the FBI to requisition the dog's corpse. We should be able to take care of it tomorrow."

"We should save the piece of marked skin before we burn it," Moncrief interjected. "Chloe and Dot may be able to get something from it and if they can't, I might."

Martinez made a noise of agreement as she typed. "It's too bad our only witness so far is a dead dog."

"Is there any reason we can't talk to it?" Moncrief inquired.

"Him. His name is Baxter," Martinez corrected her as her thumbs finished the request for Baxter's body. "And can you even hold a séance for an animal?"

"Why not?" Moncrief asked rhetorically. "Animals have souls. The tricky part is finding someone who can communicate with them on such short notice."

Martinez shrugged and started a new message. "It will be a moot point if the Mine matches the magical signature, but just in case, it never hurts to ask. Although I do feel a little silly putting in a request for a dog whisperer." After the second request was sent, a befuddled look came over Martinez's face. "If dogs have souls, does that mean there's a doggie heaven?"

"I'm not even sure there is a heaven for humanity," Moncrief said darkly, which elicited a smirk from her companion.

"In the realm of shit that people make up to feel better about their miserable state of existence, doggie heaven seems harmless enough."

A knock at the door broke their navel gazing and spurred them into action. Martinez put away the crime scene photos while Moncrief cleared her face of all expression and put on her socialite facade before answering the door. "Tracy, room service is here!" she announced cheerfully as she wrote in a generous tip and signed for the meal.

# Chapter Sixteen

Along the White Nile, The Republic of South Sudan
4th of May, 4:48 a.m. (GMT+3)

It was a warm night on the water as the repurposed passenger boat chugged upstream in the darkness. The locals called the river Baḥr al-Jabal, loosely translated as *river of the mountain* which became the Mountain Nile. The English colonizers called it the White Nile after the color of the clay-filled water to differentiate it from the Blue Nile which it later joined downstream.

The river ran through the entire country, flowing from the south out of Uganda to the north and into Sudan. In the south near the Ugandan border, it was heavily peppered with rapids, and toward the north it split into various channels in the vast swamp of the Sudd. Fortunately, this section was relatively calm although it still required a certain level of crazy to risk the occasional rapids to meet here, which was precisely why Hobgoblin picked it.

He scanned the water's edge through his binoculars, looking for any sign of his rendezvous with Garang Chuoi, or as his followers called him, the General. Shortly after South

Sudan officially became a nation separate from Sudan, the many tribes occupying the area vied for political power. Some groups felt they were deliberately left out when it came time to form a new government, even though they were on the front lines in the fight for independence. As the in-fighting grew more contentious, South Sudan plunged into civil war. In such a climate, people like the General bloomed. He sowed seeds of dissent and fueled sectarian violence in the name of justice while amassing his own power and wealth.

There was no question in Buchholz's mind that the General would show up in spite of this being only their second meeting. The weapons he had aboard were too vital to let a little paranoia get in the way, not that Buchholz could blame him for being cautious. Given the number of failed assassination attempts, a health dose of paranoia was understandable.

A flash of light caught his attention and he responded by flashing the boat's light in the appropriate rhythm. It was one of the measures the General put in place for peace of mind, and Buchholz played along, even though he thought it was silly. Shave and a haircut was too universal to pass for security.

He steered the vessel to the shore and found a makeshift pier waiting for him. The General came with an entourage of armed guards. "The rapids didn't eat you," he said in English, greeting Buchholz from behind a wall of automatic weapons. His usage was correct, but his cadence was decidedly East African.

"It tried but spit me back out. I guess I'm too gristly," Buchholz replied and threw a line to shore. The General laughed as one of his men secured the rope to the pier.

Buchholz stepped to shore but gave them plenty of space. "You have the payment?"

"Of course," the General patted his pocket. "You have the goods?"

"I wasn't taking a pleasure cruise," he said dryly. "You're more than welcome to inspect the goods on the boat, but not a single crate leaves the boat until I get paid. Agreed?"

The General liked his chutzpah and nodded. "Agreed." Buchholz couldn't understand the orders he gave to his men, but he figured it out when two of them stayed with him on the pier. *Hrm, that wasn't part of the plan…* Buchholz thought.

"I wouldn't want you to get lonely," the General explained as the rest of his entourage moved toward the boat.

"How thoughtful of you," he said, but his mind was already recalculating. He'd put the crate second from the back, banking that the General would check them all, and now he was grateful for the foresight. It bought him a little extra time to think.

Disarming and killing the two armed men shouldn't be a problem once shit hit the fan on the boat; they were standing entirely too close to him to make their guns very useful. Rookie mistake. If he did the wards right, the shetani should be trapped below deck once it was released from the crate. After it took care of the General and his men on the boat, dispatching the demon would be as easy as shooting fish in a barrel—one of his pistols was loaded with banishment bullets.

*If I did the wards right...* he repeated to himself and quickly made a plan B: if the demon came to shore before he was done with the guards, he'd jump in the water. He didn't relish the idea of a swim in the Nile at night, but the shetani he'd captured couldn't cross flowing water and he could always shoot from the river. Banishment bullets just had to make contact to work.

He slowly reached for a cigarette and offered one to each guard, but only one accepted, which was one less weapon ineptly pointed at him. "So, what do you guys do for fun around here?" he flippantly asked. They either didn't understand him or chose to ignore him, but his blasé attitude produced the desired effect. He was a joke in their eyes and therefore no longer a threat.

The seconds dragged out as he waited for the first signs of distress on the boat. It was debatable if the shots or the screams came first. Regardless, Buchholz immediately sprung into action. He dropped his cigarette and grabbed the gun of the non-smoking guard. With his other hand, he pulled out a knife and slid the blade twice into the guard's back, solidly punching each kidney.

While the other guard fumbled for his weapon, Buchholz turned his compatriot's gun toward him and pulled the trigger, unloading a series of bullets into center mass. With both men down, he took cover. The last thing he needed was to get hit by a stray bullet from someone shooting inside the boat.

He pulled out the pistol loaded with banishment bullets and waited a full minute after the screams and gunfire had stopped. It seemed like the wards had held, but he saw no need to get cocky. When he was fairly certain the shetani wasn't going anywhere, he approached the boat. It was shot to hell and taking on water, but it wouldn't be his problem in five minutes.

He made a noise to draw the demon to the warded threshold and saw an injured man pulling himself up the stairs. "*Bitte helfen Sie!*" it called to Buchholz, but he knew better. Shetani could assume the shape of animals and humans, and the chances of one of the General's guards speaking German was zero to none. He fired his weapon and an unearthly wail emanated from the body as it writhed and shifted to its true grotesque form before disappearing from the mortal realm.

With a flashlight in hand, he ventured below deck and found human remains splattered all over the cabin. He zeroed in on what looked like the General's torso and patted down the pockets until he found his payment—a velvet bag of uncut diamonds.

The sky was just beginning to lighten and he estimated he had a little over an hour before dawn. He quickly dumped the two guards he'd killed onto the deck and grabbed his concealed bug-out bag from the helm. The boat was already rigged, and he double-checked the connections to make sure they weren't damaged in the firefight with the demon.

Once he was satisfied, Buchholz stepped to shore, leaving the vessel for good. He untied the boat from the pier, gave it a hearty push, and watched the current take it away. An unabashed look of glee came across his face as he pushed the button on the detonator. The explosion lit the night sky and he watched the shock wave ripple out and across the water. There was nothing that couldn't be fixed with a little ordinance.

He found their vehicle a little ways up the footpath and drove it to his second rendezvous point of the evening. A statuesque woman on a motorcycle was waiting for him. "Is it done?"

He stared into her big brown eyes. "The General is no more."

She spat on the ground at the mere mention of his name—another butcher of Bentiu had been put down, may he burn in Hell. "Good. We are one step closer to peace."

"Peace sells, but who's buying?" he quipped as he climbed out of the jeep. He had many missions under his belt and was no stranger to the notion that peace could be obtained by killing the right person. However, it rarely worked out the way the analysts thought or the locals hoped.

"How poetic. Is it Owens?" she asked as he sat behind her on the motorcycle with a grenade in hand.

"No, it's Megadeth," he corrected her. "We should get

going. I have a flight to catch in Juba."

She pouted and gave him a sharp look. "I thought I had you to myself for a few days."

He shrugged apologetically. "I'd stay if it were up to me, but duty calls." He gave her a mischievous grin. "You know, my flight isn't until eleven. If you drive fast, we could steal away a few hours."

She fired up the engine and took off as soon as he tossed the grenade into the jeep and wrapped his arms around her.

# Chapter Seventeen

Buchholz stepped out of the Cessna and welcomed solid ground. There were no direct commercial flights from Juba, and hiring a private charter was the sensible thing to do, even if flying in a prop plane through choppy air was not his cup of tea. There was a car waiting for him on the tarmac, and the driver exited the vehicle and opened the door for the man in the back seat.

"Nalin, so good to see you again," Yazid Alaneme greeted him. "You are looking well!"

"Same to you, Yaz," he replied as they exchanged a warm handshake. "Getting a little doughy, though. Married life obviously agrees with you."

"Young women age but a good cook only gets better with time," the African spoke in aphorisms. Buchholz chuckled. It was a quirk that he'd come to appreciate during their stint together. The driver opened the spacious trunk of the sedan—a three-body trunk by Buchholz's estimation. He smiled as he deposited all but his backpack inside—Alaneme always came prepared.

His cargo was the other reason Buchholz had chartered a flight. There was only so much that fit in the concealed compartment of his Salt Mine luggage, and he was loaded for bear. Flying commercial would have meant unloading his arsenal in South Sudan and rearming in Tanzania—doable, but a pain in the ass.

"I was surprised you could come so quickly," Alaneme spoke once they were both inside the car. "I was expecting to have to wait."

"I was already in the area," Buchholz explained vaguely.

"Do I want to know why?" Alaneme asked but quickly retracted the query. "Wait, don't answer that. If I have to ask, I already know the answer." Once upon a time, he was in the same business as the German. While he chose to settle down and take a government position, Buchholz had made different choices. He motioned to the driver to proceed and raised the divide to give them some privacy.

"Why don't you tell me about your problem?" Buchholz spoke freely once the tinted bulletproof glass was up. The car started moving and the driver took the circuitous route back to the main road.

Alaneme shook his head. "It's weird, Nalin. Very weird."

Buchholz shrugged. "Weird is my specialty."

"The past few weeks, we've found a series of dead people with their rib cages open and their hearts missing," Alaneme jumped in headfirst.

A lump formed in Buchholz's throat as memories of Mictēcacihuātl's Tongue flooded his mind. One cut of its obsidian blade caused its victim's heart to burst out of their chest, hover over their head, and explode. He'd foolishly tried to wield the foot-long dagger to finish off a revenant, only to find he'd grabbed a tiger by the tail—it actually reinvigorated the undead. Mictēcacihuātl's Tongue was supposed to be in the Moncrief family vault, but if it had broken out once before....

"Were the ribs collapsed inward or outward?" he asked immediately.

Alaneme could tell from his tone it was an important distinction, even if he didn't understand why. "Crushed in. There was a witness at the latest incident. Last Friday, it killed three poachers after they shot down an elephant bull. He said an ungulate of great size stepped on them and ate their hearts, like cracking open a walnut shell to get at the meat."

"Did it eat the elephant's heart?" Buchholz asked, glossing over the rarity of an ungulate that ate flesh.

"No, but the really strange thing is that no other scavengers ate from the bodies. I've never known wild dogs or vultures to be picky," Alaneme added.

"I can see why you called me," Buchholz replied sympathetically. "Have the locals taken any protective measures?" While much of East Africa was Christian, there were still those that practiced the old ways, and Alaneme liked to consult them when odd things were afoot. He'd seen too many things to dismiss them as superstitious bumpkins.

"It seems to be avoiding communities that take precautions but the consensus among the old guard is that it is not native." Although unstated, Buchholz heard the message loud and clear—someone imported a supernatural creature into the area. He wasn't just hunting it, he was also hunting the practitioner that brought it to Tanzania.

The German's demeanor changed on a dime. The carefree confidence that bordered on arrogance turned serious and calculating. "Have you identified a pattern in the attacks?"

"Always at night and in isolated rural areas. So far, all the bodies have been found in a fifty-kilometer radius," Alaneme responded. "If it was just poachers, I wouldn't raise too much of a fuss—they can all die for all I care—but some civilians have been killed so it cannot be allowed to continue."

Buchholz parsed the odd turn of phrase; a radius implied a center point. He raised one of his dark eyebrows. "And what is at the center of this fifty-kilometer radius?"

Alaneme smiled. "A laboratory complex."

"A part of the nature reserves?" Buchholz guessed.

Alaneme laughed out loud—like they had that sort of money. "No, privately owned by a multinational corporation."

"No offense to your fine country," he prefaced, "but who the hell puts their lab in rural Tanzania next to the border of Rwanda and Burundi?"

His host shrugged. "The government is stable with high English fluency and both land and labor are cheap. Throw in some tax breaks and lax regulations, and you've got a perfect place to set up shop."

A knowing smirk bloomed on Buchholz's face—so that's why Yaz called him. His hands were tied; he couldn't use official resources to tackle the problem. He needed someone who knew how to take care of things under the table. Weird things.

"I think I understand," Buchholz reassured him and came up with the rough shape of a plan. "I'll start with what is killing people and then move on to who smuggled it into your country," he spoke in code. "I'll need maps of the area and access to where the previous attacks took place. Maybe even talk to the witness."

"That can be arranged, but we'll want to be back in the city before it gets dark," Alaneme said ominously.

Buchholz tensed. It felt like Alaneme was setting him up for something, but he played it easy. "Because that's when the beast feeds?"

"Because my wife insisted on inviting you to dinner as soon as she overheard me making plans for your arrival." His face was serious but there was a sparkle of affection in his eyes when he spoke of her.

"How much does she know about our shared past?" he asked gently. It had been years since they last worked on a mission together, and part of the reason their bond was so strong was because it was forged in blood and violence.

"Only that I wouldn't have made it home without you," Alaneme confessed. "Which is why she went straight to the market for specialty foods. She's going to make German food for you."

Buchholz could only imagine how an African woman would interpret German food, but he graciously replied, "I'll never say no to a home-cooked meal."

# Chapter Eighteen

Alan Brooks stared at the screen and reread what he'd written so far. *What everyone, including the betting establishment, failed to take into account...* He didn't know how he was going to finish the sentence, but he had to come up with something. He couldn't simply report what happened in an artful way. Thanks to the internet, the race results and colorful prose were already out there. The journal wanted a fresh angle—some insight, depth, and expert analysis that appealed to their discerning readership. And they wanted it yesterday, but he had until the end of the day.

Brooks was no stranger to turning bullshit into marmalade, but he was honestly stumped. He had a sneaking suspicion that something hinky was going on, but he wasn't dumb enough to put that in print. He had considered all the usual suspects: training style, racing stats, lineage—there was no unifying factor between the winning horses except they were all descended from Man o' War, but that could be said about nearly every racehorse in America. That legendary horse studded non-stop for decades and sired sixty-two stake winners, including the Triple Crown winner War Admiral and Seabiscuit. Genetically speaking, Man o' War was the Genghis Khan of the American racehorse.

What he needed was some factor that was easily overlooked in the sea of stats—something he could point to that would make his readers feel clever by association. It didn't have to be true, just plausible; his good name would do the rest.

The cursor flashed at the end of the incomplete sentence, taunting him until he broke the first rule of writing: he got out of his chair. He went to the kitchen and poured himself another cup of coffee; a little caffeine always helped him think. He rooted around in the cupboard and fridge to see if there was something sweet to go with his black coffee; a light snack to fuel the brain. He settled on a pudding cup and looking out the window for inspiration.

The rolling hills were inviting; it was a perfect day to hit the stables and ride the trails if he wasn't up against a deadline. Shelbyville was prime horse country with over ninety farms producing American Saddlebreds for the global market, and Brooks had no problem with having more equine neighbors than human ones. Thirty minutes outside of Louisville and an hour from Lexington, he was close enough to get what he wanted from the city while living a rural daily existence. It was the best of both worlds.

A black luxury sedan interrupted his daydreaming, and his

natural curiosity was piqued when it pulled into his driveway. He wasn't expecting anyone; maybe it was someone for his wife?

He watched a young woman climb out of the driver's seat dressed in jeans and a button-down top with an oversized leather bag. She was tall and lean, broad at the shoulders and hips with sturdy thighs. *She'd make a fine rider but too tall to be a jockey*, he absentmindedly thought as he set his cup down and readied himself for company.

The chime of his doorbell sounded and he counted to ten before answering. She gave him a warm smile that disarmed him. "Hi, you wouldn't happen to be Alan Brooks, would you?"

"Depends. Who's asking?" he answered cautiously. She was dressed too casually to be a Jehovah's Witness or a saleswoman, but one could never be too careful.

"Someone who could benefit from your expertise," Martinez said cryptically. "May I come inside and explain? It will only take a few minutes and if you're not interested, I'll be on my way." She couldn't magically compel him to help without being draconian about it, but that didn't stop her from using her God-given graces, intuition, and a little will to soften her target. She'd pegged Brooks as a man who liked a good mystery, and he would be more willing to listen if he liked her.

"Can I at least have a name?" he asked coyly.

Her smile deepened. "Tracy Martin, correspondent for the

Institute of Tradition," she introduced herself and handed him a card.

*A journalist?* he thought as he admired the selected font on her business card—tastefully feminine without being flowery or unprofessional. He didn't recognize the organization as equine in focus, which made her request even more mysterious. The grammarian in him gave her points for using "may" instead of "can," and anything sounded better than returning to that relentless, blinking cursor.

"Sure," he agreed and opened the door wide. "You caught me in the middle of a coffee break. Would you like a cup?"

"If it isn't any trouble," she answered politely. She already knew the door had no wards, but she kept an eye out for other signs of magical practice. "You have a lovely home," she commented as she followed him into the kitchen.

"That's all my wife's doing. I just live here and put my dishes in the sink and my socks in the hamper," he answered humorously as he fetched another mug. "How do you take your coffee?"

"One sugar and a splash of milk," she replied as she took a seat at the kitchen table and set her bag down. "Is your wife at home?"

"No, she's at work," he responded and placed a warm cup in front of her. "Which is what I should be doing, so it's a good thing you caught me during a break." He pulled out a chair for himself and settled in with his cup. "Now, Tracy Martin, what's this all about?"

"I need someone who can communicate with animals, and I was told you may be able to help," she laid out her request simply.

"Is this for a Derby story?" he probed. "Because I'm trying to finish one of my own at the moment."

"No, I actually need you to talk to a dog," Martinez revealed a little more.

"Anyone can communicate with a dog. The key is tone and body language," he replied generically. "And, of course, listening to what they are trying to say through their behavior."

"Yes, but not everyone can understand animals as well as you can," she pressed. Even though there was no mention of magic, it was implied, and her bluntness took him by surprise.

He laughed to disguise his nerves. "Someone is having fun with you, Ms. Martin. I'm no Doctor Doolittle, and there are plenty of people who work with dogs that would better suited to help you. I've spent my whole life around horses."

Martinez placed her cup down resolutely. "Mr. Brooks, your skills have not gone unnoticed. I simply want to employ those skills."

He narrowed his eyes and tilted his head to one side. "Who did you say sent you?"

A wry smile appeared on her lips. "I didn't, but I assure you, you aren't in any trouble. Not with me."

He didn't like the implication and unconsciously closed his

open posture. "You have a strange way of asking for help—coming into a man's home and threatening him."

"It's not a threat. It's a statement of fact," she said neutrally. "You know something fishy happened at the track last weekend. I'm just the first person who showed up at your door. You can refuse to help me, but the next person may not be so gracious. If I can produce results and tie a bow around it quickly, the people from Churchill Downs may never get around to considering you."

Brooks sat up in his chair and dropped his charade. "I didn't have anything to do with whatever you think happened. I just talk to the horses. I don't do any spells, curses, or hexes," he said defensively.

"I believe you," Martinez assured him and paused for effect. "But the next person may not."

Were it not for the earnestness in her eyes, he would have ended the conversation then and there. Even though it was unsettled, his gut told him she was on the level. He would rather deal with a straight shooter than gamble on whoever the track would send. "Where's this fur ball you need to talk to?"

"In cold storage," she answered his question directly before explaining in full. "I'm here because someone killed a dog, brought him back to life, and had him kill his owner. I need to know more in order to stop them from doing it again. Or worse."

His stomach turned sour at the thought. "And you think

that had something to do with the Derby races?"

"Maybe. Maybe not," she answered equivocally. "But either way, it's a damn dirty way to treat a dog."

Brooks grunted. He couldn't disagree with that. "I can communicate with animals, but I can't communicate with the dead," he pointed out.

"You're not the only one with special skills, Mr. Brooks," Martinez replied. "I can make the connection. I just need you there to translate."

"And if it doesn't work?" he inquired.

Martinez shrugged and gestured with her hands. "Then we go our separate ways and pretend like this never happened."

"Can you keep the track off my back?" he got straight to the point.

"I'm not part of their organization, so I can't make any guarantees, but should you come up in the course of their investigation, I can vouch for you. To shield you preemptively would only draw attention to you," she reasoned.

He looked at the wall clock and noted the time. "How long does something like this take?"

"If everything goes well, an hour or two, tops. I have everything I need in my bag. We can do it now, if you'd like," she suggested. "I just need someplace where we won't be disturbed, and where the floor is a flat surface I can mark with chalk."

"Will the garage do?"

"Probably, but we'll need a broom to clean up afterward."

Brooks motioned to a metal door on the other side of the kitchen. "Let's get this over with. I want everything cleaned up before my wife gets home, and I still have an article to finish."

The garage was packed with tools, equipment, and anything else that required storage, with just enough room to park two vehicles inside. Brooks moved his truck to give them more space and closed the garage door on reentry. The fluorescent strip lights flickered before they fully illuminated the room and Martinez got to work.

Everything started with the circle, which she made by securing one end of a length of string to the floor and making a series of arcs with the piece of chalk on the other end. She made the circle three feet in diameter—large enough for a medium-sized dog to stretch out but too small for it to gain momentum. She added some basic protection sigils just in case Baxter had gone full-on Cujo from being subject to the worst kind of necromancy.

When she was satisfied that the circle was correct, she placed personal items taken from Kinkade's home inside the circle—a ratty chew toy, a much-loved plastic rubber hamburger, and some Beggin' Strips from the cupboard. She placed candles around the outer perimeter and lit them before beckoning Brooks to join her.

"The circle will contain the dog. We are completely safe as long as we stay outside the circle and the circle isn't broken," she explained in short, declarative sentences. "Do you understand?"

Brooks nodded. "Got it. Don't touch the chalk and stay outside the circle," he paraphrased as he took a seat opposite her.

Martinez cleared her mind and summoned her will—*Hail Mary, full of grace...* She spun it in a circular motion until it was ropy from the centripetal force. Instead of creating a vortex and inviting any spirits to manifest, she looped the end like a lasso. As a hedge-level magician, Brooks barely perceived the invisible metaphysical energy, but he could see enough to be in awe of it.

Martinez sprinkled bits of fur taken from Baxter's body into the candle flame in front of her and the smell of burnt hair and caramelized blood filled the air. "Baxter? Are you there, boy?" she called in a friendly, high-pitched voice. "I brought some of your toys. Don't you want to come play?" The lasso circled between her and Brooks, looking to snare its target.

Martinez whistled and made kissy noises. "Come on out, boy. I'm not going to hurt you. I brought treats," she added and held a Beggin' Strip to the flame until it released a meaty aroma.

A cold chill cut through the garage and goosebumps erupted on Brooks's arms when he heard the faint jingle of dog tags come out of nowhere. He watched the center of the plastic hamburger depress on its own and a tentative squeak sounded, followed by more in rapid succession.

"Good boy, Baxter!" Martinez lavished praise on him and burned a little more of the treat. "I want you to meet my friend." She nodded to Brooks to introduce himself.

*Hey, Baxter*, Brooks silently communicated with the spirit inside the circle.

He immediately got a reply. *You speak dog!* Both Martinez and Brooks felt a whirl of energy circle the inner rim of the chalk, but only he understood it was from excitement.

*Sure do, buddy. My lady friend wants to ask you some questions but she doesn't speak dog,* he explained and addressed Martinez. "He's friendly. Go ahead and ask him whatever you want to know."

She breathed a sigh of relief. It wasn't proof positive, but it was unlikely that the dog was brought back necromantically. "Baxter, I want to know about who came to the house right before you died," she asked.

The air became tense and charged as the spirit of Baxter growled low. It was imperceptible to human hearing, but it vibrated through them metaphysically.

"It's okay, Baxter. She wants to stop them before they can hurt anyone else," Brooks spoke out loud for Martinez's benefit but the canine understood his meaning nonetheless.

He sniffed the air to assess the trustworthiness of those that had summoned him. When he didn't sense malicious intent, he answered with a short bark.

"The bad man that smelled of rotten eggs?" Brooks

translated.

Martinez's eyes lit up. Anyone summoning demons would have trace amounts of sulfur on them. Maybe not enough for people to detect it, but a dog's sense of smell was a whole other matter. "That's him. Good boy!"

She changed her tone and addressed Brooks. "Can you get a description for me? Age, height, hair and eye color, clothes, accessories, glasses, tattoos—anything that could help me pick him out of a lineup."

"Maybe, but it's going to take a little time. Dogs see the world differently than people. And it will go faster if I can do this in my head," Brooks added.

"That's fine. I'll keep the channel open," she answered.

Brooks embarked on a mash-up of twenty questions and Guess Who before he had anything resembling a description. "You're looking for an older heavyset man with glasses. He's bald, but his beard is brown with a fair amount of gray. His eyes are blue and he wore a pinkie ring on his left hand. No visible tattoos or scars, but he did smell of Churchill Downs as well as alcohol and cigar smoke."

"How does he know what Churchill Downs smells like?"

"He said the man smelled like his owner did when he came home from work."

"Makes sense. Was it light or dark out when he arrived at the house?" Martinez inquired. Dogs were smart and knew more words than people gave them credit for, but she doubted they could tell time.

Brooks consulted Baxter. "It was still light, but turning dark."

"Anything about his clothing?" she asked hopefully.

"Human clothes was about as far as I got, but he wasn't wearing a hat." Brooks threw in the factoid in case it was important. "There was a logo on his jacket, but Baxter didn't recognize it. The best description I could get was squiggles in a square."

She bobbed her head ambivalently and changed directions. "Had he been at the house before?"

Brooks relayed the question to Baxter in terms he could understand: *Was he a friend or stranger?* Baxter barked his reply. "First time at the house," Brooks interpreted for Martinez and asked her a question of his own. "Who's Mark?"

"His owner," she answered. "Why?" She'd gone to great lengths to tell Brooks as little as possible.

"Baxter wants to know if he's okay. What should I tell him?" Brooks asked for guidance subtextually.

"Tell him that the bad man hurt him too, just like he hurt Baxter," she stretched the truth, although technically they did both bleed out from a severed carotid artery. If Baxter had no memory of killing his owner, she didn't see any reason to burden him with such knowledge now. More importantly, this proved that Baxter's soul definitely wasn't in his body when it killed Mark Kinkade.

Martinez heard a soft whimper echo in the garage as Brooks broke the news. "I'm sorry, Baxter. There wasn't anything you could have done to stop the bad man, but I'm going to track him down. You were a good dog."

A mournful howl echoed in the garage. "Mark was a good human," Brooks translated for Martinez.

There was no way for her to pet him, so she did the next best thing. She pulled out a Hershey's chocolate bar she'd bought in case the Beggin' Strips were insufficient. She slipped it out of the paper sleeve, unwrapped the foil, and held a corner over the candle's flame. The velvety smell of vanilla and cocoa filled her nostrils. "Here you go, boy. You can have this now. It can't hurt you anymore." Baxter recognized the aroma of the forbidden treat immediately and lapped it up.

After Martinez sent Baxter's spirit on his way and severed the connection, Brooks needed a moment to compose himself. He'd never before had the chance to witness such a casual use of magic that close up. It was one thing to know that there were people out there who could do such things and another to be sitting right next to them while they did it.

Martinez put Baxter's things back in her bag and grabbed the push broom hanging on the wall. A séance wasn't particularly difficult to perform—more of an exercise in knowledge than raw ability—and she didn't want Brooks to try to replicate the ritual on his own. The chances of him pulling it off without explicit training were slim, but not impossible.

"That was nice of you, lying to the dog," he said when he finally broke the silence.

"He didn't do anything wrong," she replied, vigorously pushing the broom across the circle and smearing the chalk.

"Do you really think you can track this guy down?" he asked.

She poured a little water over the area and shrugged. "I've worked with less." He laughed at her understated delivery. Under different circumstances, he probably would have welcomed her company. "As you're a legitimate horse whisperer, let me ask you something. What do you think happened at Churchill Downs last Saturday?"

Brooks mulled it over. "I'm not sure, but I know the horses knew something wasn't right. Kept talking about running with death and their ancestors."

"And that's not normal for horses," she guessed.

Brooks shook his head. "No. There's excitement and nerves, but not fear. Not on this level. It was everywhere, but once the races were over, the horses were fine." Talking about horses put him back on solid ground, things he knew and understood gutturally. He wasn't sure what to make of all this, but maybe he could use it for his story. "What explanation do you tell people when you can't say 'It's magic; a wizard did it'?"

"In my experience, it doesn't matter what you say. People's brains will fill in the blanks to support what they want to believe, and most people don't want to believe magic is real.

Not really," she responded truthfully.

She put the broom back where she'd found it once she was certain she'd eradicated any traces of the sigils. "Thanks for your help, Mr. Brooks." She extended her hand, offering him physical confirmation that their business was concluded.

"Don't take this the wrong way, but I hope we never have cause to see each other again," he said as he shook her hand.

Martinez hoisted the bag on her shoulder and pressed the garage door open. The sunlight flooded the concrete floor and walls. "Here's hoping. Good luck with your article."

They both entered their respective vehicles, and he watched her car drive away in the rearview mirror of his truck. Then he pulled it back into the garage, cut the engine, and lowered the door.

*****

Martinez stopped for lunch in a local cafe to reset her mind and quiet her stomach. She had a soft spot for dogs, and she just about lost it when Baxter called his owner a good human. She started by reviewing the facts after this morning's séance, enumerating what was known and still unknown. Baxter's nose suggested that his reanimator was also their demon summoner. This morning, she'd gotten word from the Mine that the magical signature from Kinkade's kitchen was not in the system, but now she had a physical description. Unfortunately, it didn't fit any of the practitioners she and Moncrief had captured at brunch.

But he was there. Baxter said he smelled like the track. If she were acting on her own, she would go to Churchill Downs as FBI, obtain security tapes, and load up on snacks for the tedious work of reviewing hours of video. However, she didn't want to jeopardize the play Moncrief was making. Her source had taken the bait, and Wilson was coming in as Daniel Westwood, the heiress's magically abled private security. However, there was more than one way to skin a cat. She winced a bit at her internal monologue. *I should come up with a better saying*, she thought in light of current affairs.

While she waited for her soup and sandwich, she pulled out her phone and sent a request to the Mine's analysts: comb the social media from the Derby and look for a heavyset bald and bearded caster wearing glasses and a pinky ring. It was the proverbial needle in a haystack, but it was more than they had this morning.

By the time Martinez ate and returned to Louisville, the paperwork requesting Baxter's body from the Department of Animal Control had come through. Despite being an unusual request, they didn't dally. Schultz had already finished with her necropsy and sent the brain samples for testing. The FBI's request saved her the hassle and cost of getting rid of the body.

Because it had been brought back to life after death, the only way to be certain the reanimator couldn't rekindle the connection sometime in the future was to cleanse it with fire. Her work was made easier since necromancy wasn't involved, but cremation of the body was non-negotiable.

Setting it alight in a remote location would do in a pinch, but it was a last resort. Burning a body in a field or abandoned structure risked drawing more attention to the corpse, but if needs must, it was better than Baxter rising from the grave.

Most funeral homes had cremation services, but they had their pitfalls. It acknowledged there was a body in the first place and that required appropriate documentation. It was easy enough to bribe one's way around legalities, but that aroused suspicion as it raised the question of why said body couldn't be processed through their commercially offered service. Even if she went through the motions of acquiring fake supporting papers, the process was subject to local regulations and some states had waiting periods on cremations.

Which was why Salt Mine agents favored waste management or biohazard furnaces every time. They operated regularly, their fires ran hotter than cremation ovens, and unbeknownst to the general populace, there was usually one nearby. It was the ideal way of disposing of a body without leaving physical evidence after the fact. It was also easier to sneak a payload into a burn— no one opened a container labeled biohazard to check what was inside, which meant security was surprisingly lax as long as it was coming from a known source of biohazardous material.

Martinez collected the remains of Baxter Kinkade and

removed the arcane mark of Anubis before packing it for disposal. She put his toys, his dog tags, and the rest of the Beggin' Strips in the bag, not unlike how ancient Egyptians filled a tomb full of items they thought the dead would need in the afterlife. She observed a moment of silence before putting Baxter's remains to rest, once and for all.

# Chapter Nineteen

Louisville, Kentucky, USA
4th of May, 3:55 p.m. (GMT-4)

Marilyn Wilkes was at her desk when security called to let her know her visitors had arrived. She grabbed her ID and went to collect them. After her conversation with Ali, she'd decided to check the wards. While Wilkes wasn't officially part of the mundane security team, she never had any problems performing her esoteric duties in the shadows. With a little bit of southern charm, some media jargon, and a dollop of magic, she had access to all of Churchill Downs at any time.

Unless one was a practitioner, her work didn't look like anything special. Initially, the guards were curious about her moments of intense concentration caught on the security footage but she'd hand-waved them away, using casual sexism to her advantage. What shade of off-white they should paint the rails? There were so many to choose from…. Which vantage point should the photo be taken from? Should it be at dusk or dawn? There were so many things to consider. After a few such conversations, she didn't get questioned anymore.

Last night, she was ostensibly on the track trying to figure out how to make more advertising space for next year, but she was actually double-checking the wards. She should have been relieved when she found them intact and complete, but she wasn't. Why would Ali ask about supernatural creatures if she wasn't hinting about something being there that she couldn't say outright?

It'd prompted her to perform a full in-depth scan, and that's when she found the anomalies: ripples in the fabric of reality that suggested something magical had occurred there recently. They were very subtle, but they were there. She had no proof that it had altered the outcome of the races during Derby weekend, but her suspicions increased as when she calculated a potential fourteen different interactions—the same number as the number of races. That's when she called Ali for an assist. She wasn't one to look away out of convenience, and she liked to think her due diligence was part of the reason she got the job in the first place.

As she neared the front gate, she spied Moncrief in the company of her private magical security man. He was shorter and slimmer than she expected, but he was clean shaven, his suit of fine quality and fit, and his demeanor professional.

Wilkes put on her game face and raised the pitch of her voice to unnatural registers. "Ali, so good of you come!"

"Of course! I want to hear all about your ideas for renovating the Mansion," Moncrief replied with matching enthusiasm. They exchanged two kisses on alternating cheeks.

Wilson didn't smile or make any facial expression at her approach, but his dark eyes zeroed in on her and then away once he'd assessed her as not being a threat. Neither woman mentioned him directly as it was poor taste to address the help.

"I can't wait...I know you're going to love it! Let's get you two visitor passes and we can get started," Wilkes said, prodding the uniformed security manning the checkpoint into action. Her smile was all teeth as she cut her eyes at him.

The ladies continued their charade while they walked down the corridors with Wilson close behind. At nearly six feet tall, Wilkes towered over her guests as she led the way to the track. Once they were out in the open, she dropped the chatter but kept the smile. "It's safe to talk, but the cameras are still on."

Moncrief made proper introductions while gesturing to something in the distance. "Lynn, this is Daniel Westwood. He handles my special security concerns. Mr. Westwood, this is Marilyn Wilkes, head of magical security at Churchill Downs." They subtly exchanged nods.

"As I told Ali over the phone, I can't be certain what or when, but there is no doubt something crossed over on the track which gives me some latitude to address the situation before reporting it higher up," Wilkes began. "You can examine the area and perform diagnostic magic, but you are not allowed to change the wards in any way. Understood?"

"Yes, ma'am," he replied even though he was at least a decade her senior. There was no trace of condescension or sarcasm, so Wilkes took it as a compliment rather than a slight. It was refreshing not to have to tiptoe around a fragile male ego as she so often had to do over the course of her day.

"And it goes without saying, say nothing of what you see to anyone," she firmly insisted. It was the polite way of saying "just in case you are a complete moron, I'm going to state the obvious."

"Naturally," Wilson voiced his agreement. Westwood was a hard man of few words and slipping back into character was unsurprisingly easy for him. Of all his aliases, it was the closest to his true temperament; he could happily live in a world where no one ever talked of anything but what needed to be talked about. "Before I start, what is your objective?"

It was a loaded question, especially since Wilkes had called them before the adjudicators. She carefully crafted her answer. "I want to know how my security was breached and how to stop it from happening in the future."

With that, Wilson summoned his will and got to work. *Think, think, think...* The first thing he did was get a feel for the general framework. The bulk of the wards centered on the starting gates, but there were continuation sigils along the rails. Then, he looked closer at the runes.

Just like letters made words that formed sentences to impart meaning, the creation of wards constituted a language of its own. He wasn't skilled at computer programming, but he'd heard ward creation likened to writing code. The status of

"It Works" was the minimum requirement for something to be considered security. The ideal was streamlined instructions with minimal redundancies needed for true robustness and the utter absence of loopholes. In Wilson's experience, everyone else's wards were sloppy patchworks that had evolved over time as new threats and considerations came to the forefront. He almost never encountered systems built from the ground up.

As he unraveled each rune and teased out its meaning in the context of its relative position to the other arcane marks, he was pleasantly surprised by what he found: a coherent, thematic magical program. There was a good mix of sigils from different times and places that interlocked and reinforced each other, like a Roman tortoise formation. He could see the sewn edges, the compromises between time, effort, and cost, but they were smoothly executed and would have been invisible to most. "Who designed the wards?" he curiously asked.

"I did," Wilkes answered without breaking the pantomimed conversation she was having with Moncrief. "Why?"

The tall brunette rose in Wilson's estimation—he understood why she was so rattled that something broke through her elegant construction. "Just wanted to know in case I had questions," he replied neutrally.

The first rune he found was the trigger. While the wards were always present, their effects were not always active. There had to be a switch, something that turned on the magical protections. For example, if a house was warded against vampires, the programmed magical action wouldn't happen unless a vampire tried to cross the ward. But this trigger was less straightforward. It looked more like an electrical circuit that an on/off switch.

"The start of the race is the trigger?" he guessed as the number of nodes was the same as the number of gates.

"Yes," she confirmed. "The wards are active for the duration of the race, and the contestants are keyed based on which gate they pass through."

"Do you mind if I fire them up?" he asked permission before proceeding.

She shrugged. "Knock yourself out."

Wilson tapped a thread of his will, effectively hotwiring the wards. He noted the sequence of runes as they went live and watched the flood of esoteric activity circle the track along the guiderails, creating an invisible metaphysical shell in an otherwise open space. Sound, light, and physical objects could pass through it, but not magic or magical beings. The intent was to shield everything inside the torus from outside magical interference during the race. However, a side effect would be that it also kept any magic on the track from being perceived by those outside, which would explain how any practitioners in the stands would fail to notice a demon on the track.

He sent beads of his will down the track, checking for gaps in the protections. If there was a chink in the armor, his will would settle in the cracks. When they all returned to the starting gate after a circumnavigation, he withdrew his will from the circuit and the wards powered down.

The bulk of the runes were dedicated to magical nullification, ensuring all contestants had a clean start and a fair race. Collectively, they prohibited the expression of enchanted items worn onto the track or spells that may have been cast beforehand. Once the last horse crossed the finish line, the wards turned off and any attempted magical advantage returned *after* the winners had already been decided.

It was an innovative solution designed to curb esoteric cheating, but hardly impenetrable. The efficacy came down to what was included in the nullification wards. Wilson got down to the nitty-gritty, but the list was quite extensive. It was like reading the hazard advisories on a product insert—it seemed like overkill until you realize each one was there because at some point in time, someone had tried it.

He scanned the runes for mention of supernatural creatures and found some basic wards for elementals, fae, fiends, and undead woven into the nullification at the start of the race. *Had someone actually tried to run a reanimated horse?* he wondered. It would have endless energy, but its jockey would actually be beating a dead horse. The literalization of the metaphor was too much for him and Wilson quietly chuckled at his private joke.

"What happens to a creature that is already on the track at the start of the race if it is mentioned in the wards?" he questioned their keeper.

"It would get pushed out of the inner ring and I get a notification," Wilkes responded a little more freely, surprised that he'd gotten that far down the wards in so little time. He *was* as good as Ali promised.

"The same alarm as someone who tries to cast during the race?" He followed the wards.

"Similar, but those are keyed to the starting gate. Jockeys that happen to be practitioners may get a spell off but not scot-free."

"The casting alarm and statistical improbability aside, I don't see anything stopping someone from summoning something *during* the race. Are there any wards prohibiting the existence of supernatural creatures on the track outright that I'm missing?" he asked with surgical precision.

"There was pressure to keep costs down and many of the traditional wards were deemed unnecessary in light of the measures already in place. The consensus, which I argued against, was that the short duration of the race precluded such necessity," she answered diplomatically.

Wilson gave her a short nod that came across as "been there, done that." When it came to security, clients usually asked for the moon but wanted it done for a song. Budget aside, it wasn't always possible or advisable to secure against all things in all situations, and the kinds of wards in place spoke volumes. Churchill Downs was worried about cheaters, not demons. The only problem was that the Salt Mine was looking for a cheater using a demon.

"What's in place is sound. The problem is what is missing," he said bluntly. "The way I see it, one of two things happened. The first possibility is that something that wasn't covered in the wards was present on the track before the race started, but I find that unlikely. You've covered the usual suspects in the wards and of those missing, there aren't many that would have remained undetected. Plus, if they had tried to perform any magic, it would have triggered your alarm even if the source wasn't attributable to a starting gate."

"Correct," she confirmed his assertion. "And the second?"

"It was a horse," he stated as fact.

Wilkes broke cover and looked directly at Wilson in disbelief. "Excuse me?"

"If a supernatural creature possessed a real horse, it wouldn't get pushed out by the nullification because it wasn't on the track before the race began and your tracers would simply classify the horse as 'mount' as it passed through the gate. If the creature performed any magic during the race, your casting alarm wouldn't go off because it is only keyed to the jockey."

"*Historically*, horses don't cast spells," Wilkes sarcastically defended herself.

"I'm simply working toward your objective under your parameters," he reminded her.

Wilkes brushed aside her urge to sulk and put on her big girl pants. "Fine. What corrective actions would you recommend?"

"For starters, add horses to your casting alarm. It wouldn't stop supernatural creatures from entering within a horse, but that would at least alert you to magical interference coming from the mount. If you really want to keep creatures out, consider adding prohibition wards.

"Alternately, I've recently created a singularity-of-being ward that essentially scans for non-human entities inhabiting a human body. I could rework the ward for your unique situation and merge it into your pre-existing security. Instead of having to enumerate all the things you want to keep out, you are effectively only allowing humans and horses through the gates, which would stop anything trying to piggyback onto the track."

Wilson produced one of Westwood's cards and a pen from his jacket pocket and wrote down a number. "Here's my bid for the service."

Wilkes kept her composure, but her mind reeled at the number of zeros in front of her. *I'm working for the wrong people.*

She tucked the card into her pocket. "You've given me a lot to think about, Mr. Westwood. Ali was right; you are very thorough. I appreciate your candor but I think a step-wise approach is most prudent at this juncture. However, should the problem escalate, I'll keep your services in mind."

"I understand, Ms. Wilkes," Wilson accepted the brush off with aplomb. "For what it's worth, the work you did on the wards is very impressive. Not very many people would think to couple Dee's crook with Solomon's knot."

"Thank you." Wilkes accepted his compliment with a genuine smile. It was the kind of detail only another so skilled would recognize. An odd semi-grin broke out on Wilson's normally stoic face.

It took Moncrief a second to figure out what was going on and once she did, she couldn't look away. *Is this what constitutes as flirting in security nerd?* She felt like a naturalist catching a rare glimpse of the courtship dance of arcane geeks in their native habitat.

She reluctantly checked her phone when it buzzed with a message from Martinez. *Package received and delivered, reanimator=summoner, + ID.*

She taped out a response. *Almost done w/ wards.* "Shoot, I have to go! Are we good or do you need to stay longer?" she addressed Wilson, giving him an opportunity to extend his visit.

The moment had passed and there was no trace of the goofy grin as he nodded curtly. "I think my work here is done. You have my contact information, Ms. Wilkes."

"I do," she answered coyly.

Moncrief sighed at Wilson's missed opportunity and came in for a shallow hug which Wilkes reciprocated. "I'm only a phone call away," she said softly.

Wilkes squeezed her arm. "Thanks, Ali."

When they broke contact, Moncrief gaily added, "Give me a call when you get to Maryland. I'm planning a ladies' high tea for Aunt Bethany. You should come and help me lower the average attendee age."

"Sounds like fun. We can take turns fielding questions about why we aren't married yet," Wilkes dryly quipped. "Shall I escort you out?"

"No need. I know the way," Moncrief answered. She knew Wilson always welcomed the opportunity to poke around without supervision. She was surprised when he declined, and they headed straight for the car. He opened the door for her and took his seat behind the wheel.

"What's up?" he asked as soon as they were finally alone and free to speak.

"Martinez hit pay dirt. She's got a positive ID and confirmed the reanimator is the same person as the summoner. And she's taken care of the dog's body," Moncrief quickly relayed the gist of the text before grilling him for answers. "So, what really happened on the track?"

"I suspect the summoner used the surge of the wards firing up to finish a spell that summoned the blood demon to the horse marked with the inscribed cross," Wilson replied succinctly.

Moncrief rolled the idea around in her head until it made sense. "Someone doped the horses with a demon?"

"If would explain how long-shots overtook the favorites and

how a demonic signature appeared on the track," he pointed out as he turned on the engine.

Moncrief's analytical mind immediately starting poking holes in his theory. "But you can't pre-summon a demon. That's not how it works. They aren't partially baked bread."

"Maybe not from Hell, but what if the demon were already in the mortal realm and the spell was simply redirecting it to a specific target? That would be possible in the time frame of a race," he countered.

"How on earth did someone figure out how to use the wards to power their spell?" She moved to the next point that confounded her. "Was it an inside job? Is Lynn in trouble?"

"I don't think so," he answered her last question first. "If it were someone on the inside, it would have to be her bosses and I don't think she's in a rush to tell them what she's discovered. She seems...prudent."

In the rearview mirror, Wilson caught Moncrief's smile at his slight pause but choose to ignore it. "As for how, the wards aren't shielded, and no one would notice a small amount of power siphoned off the top. It's like someone stealing cable from their neighbor—the wards are working as intended so no one thinks anything is wrong," he theorized. "But it would take precise timing."

"Someone at the race," Moncrief voiced his thoughts.

"Exactly. And now that Martinez has an ID, it's just a matter of figuring out how deep this summoner is in with demons."

He'd put two bullets into the last rogue summoner he'd come across, and he wouldn't hesitate to do it again if the situation called for it.

*****

When they arrived at Moncrief's suite, Martinez greeted them with a name. "Dr. Karl Gossen, sixty-two-year-old German, lead geneticist at Equus International." She looked up from her tablet with a spark in her brown eyes. "Oh hey, Wilson. Good flight?" she acknowledged him as an afterthought.

He shrugged and loosened his tie. "Not bad."

"So the dog séance panned out?" Moncrief marveled as she put her bag down. "How did you get a name so quickly? Was he at brunch?"

"No, but Leader had already had the analysts make a list of repeat winners from Saturday's races. When I asked them to comb social media, they ran the physical description that Baxter provided against that first and found a match," Martinez replied.

"At least the motive is clear cut. What people won't do for money," Moncrief sighed. "The guy at brunch—he was all about breeding. I take it he wasn't talking about artificial insemination and tracking ovulation."

"Their slogan is Breed Better," Martinez informed her.

"That's not super creepy," Moncrief remarked as she took

off her heavy earrings and set them down on the vanity.

"It gets better. They have been investigated for unethical acquisition and use of stem cells, and it is speculated that they moved their lab out of the EU to avoid stricter regulations on genetic modification. And whatever you do, don't do an internet search for designer horses." She had the haunted look of someone who went too far down a rabbit hole. "Unfortunately, Karl has flown the coop. He left town Sunday morning and is already on the other side of the Atlantic."

"I would leave town too if I'd just rigged the Kentucky Derby and killed my co-conspirator with his own reanimated dog," Moncrief scoffed as she took a seat opposite her.

Martinez conceded the point with a nod of the head and finished recounting her afternoon. "Anyway, I got into his old hotel room and confirmed by salt casting."

"Did you find a demonic signature too?" Wilson piped up.

"No, but the dog smelled sulfur on him," Martinez explained her thought process. "What did you guys figure out with the wards?"

He borrowed Moncrief's even shorter explanation. "He doped the marked horses with a demon."

"Wow," was all Martinez got out initially. She had an open mind, but she didn't see that coming. "Points for creativity. It tracks with what the horse guy said: the horses were scared beforehand but fine after the race."

Wilson visually acknowledged her well-placed pun before

inquiring, "Did he say anything else?"

"Something about running with death and their ancestors," she said vaguely.

"Weird." He filed it away in case it became significant later. "Where was he keeping the blood demon if not in his hotel room?" he non-sequitured to the answer to his original question.

"Keeping?" Martinez repeated to make sure she'd heard him right.

"He thinks the demon was already here and Karl simply redirected it to a horse for the race, but in order to time it right with the wards, he would have been at the races," Moncrief explained.

"Here as in Louisville or here as in the mortal realm?" Martinez tried to gauge the scope of their search.

Wilson gave the matter some thought. "Either."

"It wasn't in the barns; we salted one of the winners and came up blank," Moncrief interjected.

"And security is actually pretty tight there," Martinez added. "No US holdings came up on the property search and his credit card only shows charges for food and the hotel, but he could have rented some place local and paid cash."

While the two of them brainstormed how to track down the location Gossen used to summon and hold the demon, Moncrief's mind grabbed onto a different facet of Martinez's briefing.

"You said there was a list of repeat winners. Do we think it's just Gossen or part of something bigger?" she posited the question.

"An arcane cabal?" Wilson speculated.

"No necessarily. Mark Kinkade wasn't a caster, and he came out ahead until he was killed. And the guy we had brunch with wasn't a practitioner either, but that doesn't mean he isn't in on it," Martinez pointed out. "Or he could have been selling the information. Gamblers don't ask too many questions about where a hot tip comes from."

"We're not here to police cheaters. If we take care of the demon summoner, that's job done," Wilson put in his two cents.

"But if it is bigger than just one guy, it wouldn't do any good to take care of the trigger man," Martinez argued. "We neutralize one demon summoner, they'll simply find another."

Moncrief's blue eyes lit up in a spark of inspiration. "I think I know how we can investigate if it's really just limited to Karl Gossen without alerting his suspicions."

She pulled out her phone and put on her socialite facade before dialing. "Justin? Hi, it's Alicia." Martinez smirked—last name not required, obviously. She waved her hand at Martinez and looked away so as not to be distracted.

"I was wondering if you have the number for that funny little man with the glasses at brunch. The one that tried to sell me a horse?" She ended the sentence on an up-pitch with just enough vocal fry to sell the fact that she didn't remember his name was Miles Henderson.

"Yes, Miles!" she exclaimed. "I was thinking Milo, but I knew that was wrong." Knowing things she didn't, no matter how trivial, generally made people more pliable because everyone liked feeling smart and helpful to her. "I'd like to catch him while we are both in the same city. Do you know where he's staying?"

She uncapped a pen and started writing the details on the hotel stationary. "Perfect, you're a peach," she praised him.

She answered his next question with a light laugh. "Of course I haven't changed my mind about buying a horse, silly! I'm thinking of investing in his company. Nothing beats good breeding, but I want an unbiased look at the company before making a decision. So not a word to anyone," she pretended to take him into her confidence. The only thing that spread faster than a secret was a rumor.

She nodded as he spoke. "That's a very kind offer, but I'm sure that won't be necessary," she wormed her way out of having a second meal with him. "Justin, I hate to be a bore, but I have to run," she cut the conversation short. "But thanks again for your help."

Moncrief hung up before he could object and added the number to her contacts before sliding the paper across the table. "While I'm arranging an audience with the good doctor via Mr. Henderson, his hotel room will be empty," she said with a sweet smile.

Martinez looked to Wilson. "I already know the hotel's layout and security."

Wilson responded nonchalantly, "Why not?"

# Chapter Twenty

Ngara District, Kagera, Tanzania
5th of May, 05:52 p.m. (GMT+3)

Buchholz hauled the last of his gear up the tree, a sturdy conifer fed by the rainy season. For his purposes, a tree stand was superior to a blind, and not just because of the cover it offered in a passing squall or the benefit of being raised off the muddy ground. It gave him a wider range of vision and kept him from going toe-to-toe with his prey.

There was no guarantee the creature would come this way, but after reviewing the map and visiting the sites of previous attacks, he'd discerned a pattern. They were all on the outskirts of wooded areas continuous with the land from the laboratory, and none of the attacks crossed fresh water, which he found particularly suggestive of supernatural origins. Real animals did not shun water.

When he used his saltcaster, he found the same magical signature at each scene. He photographed and sent them to the Salt Mine per protocol, but it wasn't really necessary for the task at hand. If it was a monster with a signature, there was a decent chance a banishment bullet would fix the problem.

He heard a vehicle approach and spied Alaneme in his binoculars. He was driving a jeep instead of the luxury sedan that fetched him from the airport. Using a guideline he'd secured along the trunk, Buchholz quickly scrambled down and signaled to his friend.

Alaneme parked and did a three-sixty once he was out of the car, committing the landmarks to memory should he have to find it again. Old habits died hard. "Are you sure this is going to work?"

"No, but this thing isn't going to die if we don't try to kill it," he reasoned. "Did you have any trouble getting what I asked for?"

Alaneme unhooked the back and showed Buchholz his haul. "One recently slaughtered goat, two pints of human blood packed in ice in a cooler, and a bottle of holy water."

"Excellent! Help me get the goat out," he asked his friend for an extra pair of hands.

Buchholz looked up at his tree stand and situated the corpse in just the right spot before spreading it wide open. Then he sliced open the bags of expired donated blood and liberally poured it on the goat. It was as close as he was going to get to bait without staying on the ground himself.

"I get what this is for"—Alaneme gestured to the macabre display—"but why the holy water?"

"It's never a bad idea to have some holy water on standby," he paraphrased Deacon, the Salt Mine agent who'd trained him.

Alaneme couldn't find fault with the sentiment. "Are you sure you don't want me to stay and back you up?"

"And risk making your lovely wife a widow after she made me rouladen with spaetzle and German chocolate cake for dessert?!" he replied. He didn't have the heart to tell her German chocolate cake was actually an American invention; it tasted good all the same. "Don't worry, Yaz. I'll be in that tree with enough firepower to bring down a herd of charging rhinos. And there is a good chance I'm just going to spend the night in the rough."

"Okay, but call if something goes sideways. I can get here in half an hour," Alaneme offered.

"Will do," he agreed, even though he knew that wouldn't be necessary.

Alaneme closed up the back and handed him a large brown paper bag from the passenger seat. "I almost forgot; Mila made you some sandwiches. And there's probably some cookies and other things in there too."

Buchholz accepted the sack. "Thank her for me."

Alaneme climbed behind the wheel and turned the key. The engine roared and quieted when he put it in gear. "Good luck, Nalin," he bid his friend before driving away.

Buchholz climbed up to his perch and double-checked his gear before he lost the light. His binoculars were around his neck, as well as an array of knives and small firearms on his person. Laid out along the length of the solid branch was the Mubariz variant of the Istiglal IST-14.5 anti-material rifle.

The Istiglal—which meant "independence" in Azerbaijani—was invented by Telemexanika zavodu, a subsidiary of the Ministry of Defense Industry of Azerbaijan. He'd become familiar with it during his time in West Asia, and the lighter, fifteen-kilogram Mubariz variant was now his go-to sniper rifle. It could be dissembled into two separate components for transport. It operated reliably in shitty weather, dirty conditions, and temperatures between 50 to -50°C. As a bonus, it was fairly easy to find 12.7×108mm ammunition in most of the places he operated.

Each magazine held five rounds, and he packed the first with what he called a royal flush—an array of banishment bullets from five different cultural regions. It didn't matter where he was or where the creature originated from, it was bound to react to one of the banishment sigils etched in gold along the side of the custom munitions. He had put it in auto-fire so that all he had to do was point and pull the trigger to unload all five bullets nearly simultaneously. If it was still standing after he'd emptied the first magazine, he would move to Plan B: armor-piercing incendiary rounds in single-fire mode. He wasn't lying when he told Yaz not to worry.

When his final gear check was complete, he broke into the brown bag and found enough food to feed three men. *No wonder Yaz has gotten thick*, he joked as he fished out the first sandwich. He ate to a gorgeous sunset that was the most vibrant shades of tangerine and pink with streaks of backlit clouds. When he found a thermos full of hot coffee, he kissed it and helped himself to a cup. "God bless, Mila," he toasted her as he helped himself to a packet of cookies.

As darkness set in, the countryside transitioned into night and Buchholz fell into a holding pattern of waiting and watching. He was no stranger to hunting, and this was one arena where he had all the patience in the world. They call man the most dangerous prey, but that was not true in his experience; at least not since he'd joined the Salt Mine.

It was a little after ten when he saw something in the distance in his binoculars. It was a quadruped without any horns and heading in his general direction. Based on the range finder and reticle in the left eye, it was over six feet tall and a mile out. It trotted along with diagonal pairs of legs striking the ground in a two-beat gait that turned into three-beat canter as it got closer to the staged goat. It was hungry and going straight for the bait.

He switched out his binoculars for his sniper rifle but kept his finger off the trigger. The closer it was when Buchholz took his shot, the better his chance to hit—although at this range he'd be embarrassed as hell if he missed. When it came time to shoot, he calmly breathed in and out and squeezed the trigger. The rifle kicked hard against his braced and padded shoulder as he emptied the magazine into center mass.

A horrific screech rang out from the creature and he felt a familiar chill run up his spine—he'd successfully banished something. However, the ungulate was still in the mortal realm and somehow very much alive. It did an about-face and took off at a full gallop.

*Shit!* Buchholz cursed. Anything living would be toast after taking five fifty-caliber-comparable bullets, which could only mean one thing: it was undead. He grabbed Plan B, loaded, and fired. The creature fell in the bright flash as the explosive went off in a fireball. The ground was wet, but there was plenty of flesh to fuel the fire.

Buchholz slung his magical kit over one shoulder, grabbed the guide rope, and hit the ground running. He had a limited time to isolate his undead prey. When he got there, he saw the bloody and raw remains of a horse on its side. He quickly etched a rough circle around the body. It didn't have to be perfect as long as it was complete.

He popped open a canister of salt and lightly filled in the shallow trench. Then, he unscrewed the bottle of holy water and backfilled the ring of salt. With the basic security measures in place, he summoned his will—*was mich nicht umbringt, macht mich stärker.* It was only then that he could see the creature for what it was—a trapped soul.

Buchholz knew it was simply a matter of time before the arcane marks than anchored the soul to the body would burn away in the fire and release the tortured spirit. He moved toward its head so it could see him. Buchholz wanted it to know it wasn't going to die alone. He saw it and he didn't look away. It was the beginning of making a connection.

It weakly lifted its head, and Buchholz recognized a whirl of pain, torment, and anger as he stared into its large bulbous brown eyes. Empathy wasn't his strong suit, but he gutturally understood all those. He was fueled by a ball of fury buried deep inside him like the molten core of the earth itself. It was a fire that never went out. It was always with him, but he kept it locked it away. He refused to let it consume him.

But he needed this creature to know that he understood its rage, so he cracked the door open and let a little heat through. He saw in his mind's eye the numerous scenes he'd had to clean up after the fact: the acrid smoke that stung his eyes and the smell of decaying flesh as it burned. He heard the unending shriek of a mother's wail as she watched her child dismembered in front of her. It was universal, transcending language or culture. All too often, it was followed by deafening silence when someone took her life as well. He remembered the feeling of squeezing the life out of someone with his bare hands, staring into their eyes when the spark of life went out, watching the end of their everything. It was the reason he preferred guns and explosives whenever possible.

There was an agonizing cry when the spirit left the body, and Buchholz felt a flaming ball of anguish press against his impromptu circle. He had one shot to make this work.

He held all those memories close and infused them in his words and will. "You are no longer bound to this body. You are no longer bound to its pain, physically or spiritually. I will find whoever did this to you, and I will make sure they can never do it again. But your part in this is finished. Be at peace and run free."

The spirit whipped around inside the rough circle, torn by conflicting desires. It wanted vengeance for all the pain inflicted upon it, but it also wanted to run the endless plains it was made to run. It took the measure of Buchholz and decided he was a man who understood the importance of these things.

It sounded a high-pitched whinny, verbalizing its acceptance of his promise. The fire leapt high into the sky as it crossed over, unburdened by the pain of second life after death, and just like that, the spirit was gone, leaving Buchholz alone in the mud.

He immediately shut the door on the endless depths of his anger and moved away from the fire. He wiped his eyes and gathered kindling and fallen wood from nearby to feed the fire. The spirit was gone but the body still had to be cleansed, and it would take hours to burn without accelerant. He would stand vigil until there was nothing left but bones and ash.

He pulled out his phone and made a call. He was too tired to do the time zone math, but it didn't matter. LaSalle worked 24/7.

"LaSalle," the crisp tenor answered.

"It's Hobgoblin. We've got a necromancer. The spirit has been taken care of and I'm burning the body now. I sent a magical signature earlier today and I'll send you coordinates of my exact location once I get off the phone," he reported mechanically.

LaSalle took the news of a forbidden magic in stride. "I'll inform Leader. Did you get the necromancer?"

"Not yet, but I know the creature came from a nearby research facility," he replied.

"The name?" LaSalle never used three words when two would do.

Buchholz stared at the burning remains and answered, "Equus International."

"Stand by for further instructions. I'll be in touch," LaSalle replied before hanging up.

Sometimes magics were forbidden because they literally threatened the fabric of reality, like time magic. Others earned the designation because they were unequivocally wrong, and such was the case with necromancy. Its real danger was what it introduced into the world and what it normalized in the practice of magic.

Some would split hairs and say this tortured animal wasn't technically necromancy because it was a horse and not a person, but that's not how Buchholz saw it. He'd looked into its eyes. Whoever did this deserved the shitstorm he was going to shower down upon them.

# Chapter Twenty-One

Equus International Research Facility, Ngara District, Kagera, Tanzania
8th of May, 10:52 a.m. (GMT+3)

Dr. Karl Gossen stood on the terrace of Equus International Research Facility overseeing the setup for lunch. The terrace took up nearly the entire roof of the residential portion of the complex and was one of the many amenities used to lure the necessary scientists, technicians, and staff to live and work so far from civilization. Normally it was abandoned during the rainy seasons, but Gossen had arranged for a grand tent to shelter his guest from the daily drizzle. Dining al fresco with picturesque views and the patter of soft rain was just the sort of backdrop he wanted to sell Alicia Moncrief on the bigger dream of Equus International.

When the servants had finally laid out the table to his exacting instructions, he chomped down his Zeno Platinum cigar and scanned the horizon with his hunting binoculars. A humorless smile formed when he saw the small, telltale dust cloud. There were three vehicles approaching on the road from Kigali International Airport in Rwanda: the transport arranged by her own security and two armored SUVs he'd sent just in case. A potential private investor of her caliber didn't come often, and he wasn't leaving anything to chance.

When he got the news of her interest, he didn't waste time. Although her secretary had been very clear that Ms. Moncrief could not finalize her decision to invest without a tour of the facilities, Gossen suspected the visit was perfunctory based on the fact that she'd agreed to come on such short notice. He doubted the rural highlands of Tanzania was much of a vacation destination for a young heiress, and he'd convinced himself this trip was largely to determine the *amount* of her investment.

The next two days were crucial. If he played his hand right, he could be on the receiving end of a few extra hundred million—that would more than make up for the recent catastrophe with his prized experiment. Now that he had irrefutable proof of concept, he could use a new whale investor to scale up his operations and finally generate some serious money. Maybe he'd finally be able to retire as one of the richest people in the world.

"She's here," he announced to his assistant. "Notify the others and get the luggage cart." He lowered the binoculars and placed them back in their waterproof case. The rest of the terrace was abuzz with activity as he stubbed out his cigar and straightened his clothes. Instead of his normal chinos and t-shirt under a white lab coat, Gossen was wearing a suit, albeit linen with a mandarin collared shirt and no tie. There was no point in trying to pretend that Africa was Europe, and he would just sweat his way through a proper three-piece.

Gossen and his assistant descended to the ground floor and waited for the three SUVs to pull into the covered circular driveway. He nervously adjusted his glasses and twisted his pinky ring before forcing his hands to his side. It was showtime—time to project absolute confidence. He pulled his shoulders back and plastered a warm smile on his face.

A small, well-dressed man exited from the driver's seat of the middle SUV, and for a brief second, Gossen questioned the informality of his own attire but he pushed aside such thoughts. It wasn't like he could change now.

Wilson did a quick assessment of the scene before opening the back passenger door. Gossen noted the thickness of the door—T7 or T8 armored protection, a step up from the T6 of his escort vehicles. *Only the best for a Moncrief,* he thought as he watched Moncrief emerge from the vehicle in the latest designer adventure wear. He had no idea there was such a thing as safari chic, but the heiress was a vision in khakis and excess pockets. He suddenly felt better about his suit, but the thought that maybe he'd misjudged her seriousness flashed through his mind.

"Welcome to Tanzania, Ms. Moncrief. Dr. Karl Gossen," he held out his hand and introduced himself once she'd fully exited.

They shook hands and she politely replied, "Glad to make

your acquaintance, Dr. Gossen." She lowered her Valentino Butterfly sunglasses and flashed him her dazzling blue eyes before panning the landscape. "I must confess, I've never been to this part of the world. It's simply beautiful."

Wilson closed the door and unloaded Moncrief's extensive luggage onto the cart manned by Gossen's assistant. Even though they were staying a single night, Moncrief never travelled light. Part of it was strategic, but she also legitimately worried about not having something she might need. It wasn't like she had to worry about baggage restrictions on her G650.

Once the luggage was unloaded, Gossen paused their exchange of pleasantries and addressed Wilson. "You can park the car with the others." He raised his arm and pointed to the parking lot to the side.

"That won't be possible," Wilson said firmly. "The vehicle will remain at the front of the building for immediate access as long as Ms. Moncrief is on premises." Gossen stiffened and straightened his thick glasses; he wasn't unaccustomed to being told what was going to happen at *his* facility.

"Please forgive Mr. Westwood. He's ever so blunt and simply no fun, but that's what I pay him for," Moncrief indirectly voiced her support for her security man.

Gossen swallowed his pride. "Certainly. Why pay for expert advice if you don't listen to it?" he genteelly acquiesced. He turned to Wilson. "The vehicle can remain in the front, but it needs to be moved far enough from the entrance so workmen can easily dolly goods in and out." His tone was direct and final—as far as he was concerned, the matter was over. Wilson quickly reparked the car and joined them as they entered the building.

Wilson's dark brown eyes took everything in as they walked into the front foyer toward the bank of elevators. "I thought we'd start with lunch on the terrace," Gossen informed them as he pressed the button for the top floor. "I've taken the liberty of inviting the executive staff so we can all get to know each other. Afterward, they've created a presentation on what Equus International is now and what it could be with additional investment."

"And for Mr. Westwood?" Moncrief inquired.

"I've arranged a full tour with our chief of security," Gossen assured her. Her secretary was adamant over the phone—Ms. Moncrief did not invest in private endeavors without them being checked out by her security expert.

Moncrief smiled and gave him a slight nod. The small gesture of approval pleased Gossen beyond measure. When the elevator opened, he led her to a long table laden with a mix of Western and African foods and a collection of executives awaiting her arrival.

Wilson stayed with Moncrief until they took their seats, at which point he was dismissed with a sandwich. He made use of Gossen's binoculars and did a perimeter check from the rooftop. The Mine had provided satellite images of the surrounding terrain and he found them consistent with what he was seeing on the ground.

The seventy-acre complex was composed of three buildings forming a wide U shape. The residential and services building was on the eastern side, the laboratories were on the western, and the manufactory and animal husbandry facility formed the bottom part of the U on the southern side.

The courtyard was divided into various pens that let out into a large shared field. The open end of the U was closed off by a tall concertina-wire-topped metal fence with several different gates. To Wilson, it made sense to exercise the subject animals in a secure area because there were wild predatory animals lurking in rural Tanzania.

Once he got the general layout, he mentally noted the location of all the exterior doors as well as camera coverage. From his vantage, there were only two units on the corners of the U capturing the courtyard and the buildings behind it. All in all, everything he'd seen indicated a severe lack of surveillance.

He heard someone approach and take a stance to his left. "It's a remarkable facility," a soft voice next to him said in heavily accented English.

Wilson lowered the binoculars and looked at the speaker. He was a thin, dark-black-skinned man dressed in field clothes, unlike the executives in their suits. On his hip was a Browning HP. "John Nkwabi, chief of security," he introduced himself.

"Daniel Westwood," Wilson replied, shaking the man's outreached hand. It was calloused but smooth. "Personal security for Ms. Moncrief."

"Pleased to meet you," he said courteously. He wasn't sure what to make of the serious, intense man in the suit and tie and guardedly asked, "What do you think so far?"

Remaining in character, Wilson answered bluntly. "The electronic security here is pathetic."

Wilson's honesty took him by surprise and a sharp laugh burst out of Nkwabi, drawing looks from the executives at the table before they returned to their conversation. The chief of security relaxed a little. He could work with a man that spoke his mind. It was the ones who only said things others wanted to hear that were difficult.

"You are correct. There is little need for electronic security when you are surrounded by kilometers of empty land." He waved his arms expansively to prove his point. "Here, we don't protect against a thief or a burglar; we prepare for two jeeps of armed men."

\*\*\*\*\*

Moncrief stood silently next to her tower of luggage while Wilson checked her suite for bugs or cameras. She'd spent the afternoon in meetings and presentations with a short walk through the facilities, and all she wanted to do was relax and change for dinner. Nonetheless, she waited patiently for the all-clear.

"We're clean," he said softly and put the bug-detection equipment back in his luggage in the adjoining room.

"I kind of feel like checking for real bugs," she muttered sourly, picking at the coarse bedsheets.

Her suite was the equivalent of a two-star hotel and twice the size of his room. He smirked at her joke-not-joke and wondered when the last time was she'd spent the night in anything less than four-stars. "I'm sure everything's fine. Infesting a potential investor is a bad business decision. Just think of it as roughing it," he teased her as she began unearthing everything she would need to get ready for dinner. "Find anything concerning?"

"Boring, but nothing sinister," she sighed. She found Gossen easygoing and congenial with impeccable manners. If she hadn't known about his arcane proclivities, she would have found herself liking the man. "What about you?"

"There are a lot of security guards, but they direct most of their attention outward. They are focused on external armed threats. The interior should be dead at night and there's a paucity of electronics," he reported.

"We're sticking with the plan?" she asked for clarity.

"I see no reason not to," he agreed. "Incidentally, I've given their chief of security a list of upgrades that would have to be installed before I could even consider giving it the green light."

Moncrief smiled and nodded. Part of the reason she got to remain the fun socialite was because Wilson was so good at playing his role. "Good. They'll spend all night trying to wine and dine me, and I'll be sure to wear them out." She knew how to be utterly exhausting in the most charming way when the need arose. "Now shoo," she instructed him and gestured to herself. "It takes time to make all *this* happen."

# Chapter Twenty-Two

Wilson's phone buzzed its alarm and he groggily reached over, turned it off before resting it on his chest. He'd called it an early night after dinner because he knew this was coming, but that didn't stop him from taking a few minutes to gather his energy before rolling out of bed fully dressed. The seven-hour time difference between Detroit and Tanzania took its toll.

Unlike Moncrief, he'd only brought one piece of luggage, the one issued to him by the Salt Mine. He hadn't bothered to unpack it and tonight went straight for the concealed catch. A small wooden box fell out of the hidden compartment. Inside were two magical items from the sixth floor. The first was a hag stone: a circular piece of granite about the size of a half-dollar which had a naturally made hole in its middle. He slipped it into his pocket for when he needed a better look at what was going on esoterically.

The second item was the Anubian Gate: a silver necklace with a dangling golden Eye of Ra, but instead of where a solid gold pupil should be, there was a mummified jackal's eye held in a golden filigree cage. He shivered as he put it over his head, feeling the cold touch of the land of the dead lurking behind the unblinking iris. He would have preferred to keep in his pocket, but accidentally losing it was not an option. Once around his neck, the eye started moving in its cage. He tucked it under his shirt to ensure it couldn't see any living creatures while he wore it.

He closed the luggage and rolled the lock tumblers into sequence to activate the swap between coterminous extradimensional spaces: 1776, 1989, and then 2001. His small carryon became a full-sized suitcase, and his clothing was exchanged for all the high-tech gear he'd left at the 500, his fortified home in Detroit.

He'd packed for infiltration like Moncrief did for a weekend soiree. When he'd planned for the mission, he had no idea the place would be so woefully undersecured and he had to hunt through the tech trove for the RFID card duplicator. Most of the locks he'd come across on the tour were simple RFID locks, and he'd worn an RFID receiver all day to record the signals coming off the cards of all the staff.

He attached a universal plug adapter into the duplicator before plugging it into the wall. As it warmed up, he placed his receiver on top and quickly duplicated six thick white cards: Nkwabi, Gossen, and four of the other executives he'd gotten close to at lunch. He only intended to use Gossen's card but collected the others in case there was a recalcitrant door. He labeled each with a single letter in black sharpie before tying them together with a zip tie and stashing them in a tight black dress sock to prevent them from accidentally knocking against each other.

Then, he unearthed two brick-like objects with matching universal plug adaptors. The first was an electromagnet and the second was an EMP generator draped in a large piece of Faraday fabric. Both were wall pluggable and with them he'd be able to wipe any electronic storage he encountered, first with a powerful magnetic field followed up by the localized EMP. Any necromantic research stored electronically would be destroyed. It wouldn't affect remote storage, of course, but that side of the mission was for the Mine's hackers to figure out.

For the low-tech stuff, he slipped his everyday-carry lock pick set into his pocket next to the hag stone and his small black backpack containing three one-pound packages of salt and a roll of extra-large plastic baggies. He ran over his gear one last time before magically swapping his luggage back to carryon size.

The mission was two-pronged. The first goal was to determine if there were any other practitioners besides Gossen at the facility. After yesterday, both he and Moncrief felt confident there weren't. The second part was to locate and cleanse all traces of necromancy using the Anubian Gate. Leader didn't want to destroy the facility, but she would if there was no other way to remove the site of its taint.

Before heading out he used the toilet—no one was sneaky on a full bladder—and once outside of his room he headed straight for a particular section of the animal husbandry wing Nkwabi had excluded in his tour. It wasn't very large, just a short hallway with a few rooms labeled "laboratories" on the floorplans the Mine had acquired for him when it had hacked the Tanzanian Buildings Agency. If this was the location of Gossen's arcane practice, it meant Nkwabi either knew what was going on or was charmed. *Or both*, he mentally added.

The halls of the facility were dark and empty, and he had no difficulties avoiding the few areas that had camera coverage. The only guard he encountered on the way was the one he'd anticipated behind the front desk in the residential area foyer. The guard's head was down, completely engrossed in a book, and Wilson simply snuck by without resorting to magic.

Once he turned the corner from which he'd been deftly herded away on the tour, he understood why Nkwabi and everyone else at Equus International ignored the hall: there was a sigil of absentmindedness inscribed on the metal door at the end of the short corridor. In a way, it was the magical equivalent of the mundane Doorway Effect, amplifying a person's natural neurobiological reset when they crossed a threshold.

Given the layout of the building, it allowed Gossen to screen off the entire area with minimal magical expenditure. Any staff that saw it would forget why they were there and immediately turn back, forgetting they'd ever encountered the door and its sigil in the first place.

Wilson felt its magic tug on him, but a trained mind could easily deflect it. Nonetheless, he steeled his will and cautiously approached the door; perhaps what lay beyond was more troublesome. The power of the sigil increased with each step, and he double-checked the door for magical alarms. When he found none, he pressed Gossen's RFID card against the receiver and the lock clicked.

As the door swung open, a blast of apathy hit him from a sigil made out of black floor tiles set against the white background ones. Prepared for a secondary defense, he effortlessly sliced through it with the razor of his summoned will. It was another low-cost measure that yielded high results against non-practitioners and perhaps magicians of limited skill.

Beyond the sigil was a large laboratory that looked much like the others he'd seen on the premises except there were only two computers at the lone workstation rather than a bank of them as in the more accessible labs. On the far end of the room was another RFID keyed door leading deeper into the lab, but Wilson focused on the task in front of him: wiping the memory on the computers. Gossen was a tidy man, which made it easy to drape the large piece of Faraday fabric around all the electronics before setting off the EMP. Once his gear was returned to his pack, he opened the door to the adjacent room.

The cloying smell of decaying flesh drifted out of the

dark room, and the light that spilled inside illuminated two churning HEPA air filters on either side of a bookshelf. He flipped the nearby light switch and unconsciously augmented himself at the sudden rattle of metal on metal. He jumped back into the computer room with his weapon drawn faster than the human eye could follow.

As the florescent strips flickered on, he saw the source of the noise. Chained to the far wall were two naked zombies, a male and a female. Between them, yet out of their reach, was a zombie baby in a cage. It was barely old enough to crawl and the cage was bound in a magic circle. They moved their mouths but no sound emerged. The vocal boxes of all three had been removed but that didn't stop them from trying to moan at the proximity of Wilson's living flesh. The little one's eyes rolled wildly with excitement at the promise of fresh meat.

Their desire for flesh confirmed they were prisons for human sprits and not simply animated corpses. He shaped his will into a shield against the taint radiating from the trio; their mere presence was corrosive to a living soul.

He kept his pistol pointed at them even though the chains and cage seemed sound. Using his left hand, he fished out the Anubian Gate from under his shirt. The darting jackal eye spotted the female zombie first, and a hazy gray ray shot forth from the eye to the center of her forehead. Slowly the spirit within was separated from its shell and sucked back into the land of the dead where it belonged. The Gate did the same to the male zombie, and Wilson felt the psychic emanations pressing against his metaphysical protection lessen considerably as each body flopped to the ground, bereft of its animating force.

Wilson waited for the ray to connect with the baby zombie but the eye just darted around, rolling in its golden cage. *Why can't it see the baby?* he wondered as he put the pendent back under his shirt and pulled out the hag stone. He held the stone to his eye and the color of the world went flat like an old sepia-tinged photograph except for that which was magical. He immediately started counting the seconds: *one, two, three…*

The circle around the cage was lit up like a carousel, which meant it was magically active. While he still had time left on his ten seconds, he quickly glanced around the room for enchanted items, making a mental note of two of the books on the bookshelf. *Seven, eight, nine…* He pulled the hag stone from his eye and tucked it back into his pocket.

The baby zombie watched him walk away and mouthed in vain. Wilson could only imagine how grating the wail of an undead baby would be. It seemed contained for now and he wanted to take care of the books the hag stone had flagged. He sent out a thread of will and gently poking the enchanted books to see if anything stirred. With gloved hands, he removed a large plastic bag and emptied a good portion of one of the salt packages into it before gently pushing the books inside. Then, he put the remainder of the salt in and sealed the bag. It was far from a containment box, but it would dampen them until he could get them back to Moncrief.

He perused the remaining shelved books, starting with the ones that looked the newest and hit pay dirt on the third: a handwritten journal in German dating back three decades. As he flipped through, he recognized occult diagrams and sigils focusing on necromancy and blood magic, both old disciplines that had fallen out of favor and were considered intrinsically reprehensible by some modern practitioners.

He added it and its two more-recent companions to his backpack. It was Chloe and Dot's job to untangle the work and figure out how Gossen had mixed necromancy, demonology, and blood magic to fix a horse race, and these would be vital since he'd erased everything stored electronically. He perused the unlabeled leatherbound tomes and added a final volume—an illuminated Latin *Picatrix*. The lovely translation of the Arabic work looked to be pre-1600s and was for his own personal collection, replacing his existing twentieth-century copy.

He secured the full bag in the backpack and turned his attention to the circle. He was fully read into all aspects of the case and had his suspicions on why the zombie baby had escaped the gaze of the jackal's eye: Gossen had bound a demon into it.

Wilson approached the circle and squatted, looking eye to rolling eye with the infant zombie. "If you would like me to free you, tap the cage four times in a row," he said, testing his theory.

A normal zombie was superior to a reanimated dead body in many ways, but neither were receptive to communication from anyone except its creator. If it responded to Wilson's instructions, something else was in there. Something intelligent.

The zombie's bloodshot eyes filled with blackness as it struggled to touch the cage four times, but Wilson had his doubts that it was really as weak or uncoordinated as it appeared. Gossen had placed it in a cage for a reason and from what Wilson had seen of his magical security, the doctor didn't over-engineer.

Wilson retrieved his lock pick set and pricked the tip of his forefinger with the point of the safety razor blade he kept between two pieces of leather. A single drop formed as he gathered his will. *Think, think, think...* As he built up power, it became obvious to whatever was inside the zombie baby that Wilson wasn't going to physically break the circle. Frustrated, it violently thrashed back and forth against the bars of its cage.

Wilson smiled and brought out the Anubian Gate. Then, he forcefully declared, "With this sacrifice, I sever your binding to the mortal world!" He flung the single drop of blood from his finger and his will crashed down. As the blood passed the threshold of the circle, the demon was banished and the circle powered down. A gray ray immediately sprang out of the jackal's eye and the poor soul that was trapped in the decomposing baby was slowly freed from its torturous prison.

With all the necromantic energy removed, the Gate went

back under his shirt and Wilson did his final check: he salt cast to see if there was another magical signature. When he only found Gossen's and the blood demon's, he knew his night's work was done. This was all on Gossen and an old adage crossed his mind with a slight modification. *Suffer not a necromancer to live.*

Wilson kicked the enchantment out of the salt and lowered his soul protections. He turned off the lights and left everything else as he found it. Only Gossen would know if anything had been disturbed, and Moncrief had ensured his attention was drawn elsewhere. He took a moment to center himself before heading back. Some days, the job was harder than others.

The first thing he did when he returned to his room was knock on the connecting door. Despite the early hour, Moncrief immediately opened it. She knew it was bad as soon as she saw his face. "Do I want to know?" she asked.

Wilson was too tired to try to guess what she did and didn't want to know and simply told her the truth. "He'd trapped three souls into zombies, one of them a baby that he used as demon storage."

"Sonofabitch," she swore.

"I took care of it," he replied. "But I need you to contain these." He handed her the plastic bag containing the two enchanted books in salt.

She opened the lead-lined suitcase she'd emptied of clothing earlier. Her just-in-case outfits that had been there were now miniature-sized thanks to her magical doll's blanket. From the outside, the suitcase was identical to her other luggage, but it was the only one suitable to contain unknown magical items. Wilson placed the entire package inside and used the padded velvet partitions to keep it from knocking around.

She shut it and sealed it with her will. "So, we're a go for tomorrow?"

Wilson nodded. "I'll send my update to the Mine, but I don't expect a change."

There was something so utterly grim in his demeanor that Moncrief had the sudden urge to soothe him. Before she could think about it, she reached out and gave him a hug. To both their surprise, he let her for a few seconds before pulling away.

"Get some rest. We have an early start tomorrow," he advised before he went to his room and closed the door.

# Chapter Twenty-Three

Equus International Research Facility, Ngara District, Kagera, Tanzania
10th of May, 8:52 a.m. (GMT+3)

*Finally*, Gossen thought as Moncrief and her bodyguard exited the elevator. All of his people were anxious to secure a deal, especially after the marathon Moncrief had made them run last night. She was exhaustive, erudite, and never missed an opportunity to turn one of his men's off-hand comments into a serious point that warranted dissection. In spite of her appearance, demeanor, and age, he begrudgingly had to admit that she was perhaps the shrewdest person he'd negotiated with in a long time. He was no stranger to wooing investors, but even he was at his wit's end by the time they'd agreed to call it a night. After all that effort, she still had to sleep on it!

After she went to bed, Gossen had reassured the executives that she hadn't come off the hook yet and rallied them for one more charm offensive at breakfast. It was their last chance to win her over and their breakfast performance was going to be the difference between a modest investment and a game-changing one.

It was a glorious morning: clear blue skies without the clouds that would inevitably form later. The tent flaps were raised, letting in the cool breeze as the day warmed. Soon they were discussing the nuts and bolts of a potential arrangement over eggs benedict with fluffy *vitumbua* as a sweet side.

Once Moncrief had been safely deposited at breakfast, Wilson left and readied for their after-breakfast departure. When he returned, he ate his breakfast on the edge of the terrace, looking out at the long plain heavily dotted with acacia. He listened as the executive team talked numbers and funding schedules, and he didn't need to look to know all eyes were on Moncrief, even though it was Gossen who sat at the head of the table and she to his left.

"So we have a deal?" Gossen pressed loudly. Wilson passed by Moncrief and stood fifteen feet behind her. The visual display was enough to remind Gossen of his place and he sat back in his seat, giving her more space.

Moncrief tilted her head up and spoke. "Provided that the security is improved and all the final financials pass muster with my accountancy team, I think—"

Before she could finish her sentence, Gossen's head suddenly exploded in a shower of pink debris, covering everyone at the table in some variation of blood, bone, or brain. Everyone fell silent until they had time to process what had happened. Then the screaming started.

"Sniper!" Wilson yelled, pulling Moncrief from behind

and away from the headless corpse that had toppled over from the impact. Using his body as a shield, he guided her behind the elevator superstructure, where he pressed the button and drew his Glock, pointing it at the stunned executives as they started to seek the same shelter.

"Stay back!" he yelled, "No one comes close to Ms. Moncrief! We are out of here!"

The executives scrambled at the sight of Wilson's Glock. Some hugged the ground while others darted for the stairs on the far side of the terrace. Two managed to tip the table for cover in a crash of silverware and breaking flatware. It didn't matter that no one knew where the shot came from—any cover felt better than none.

Moncrief allowed Wilson to shepherd her to safety, into the elevator and through the foyer into their armored rental car. Once they were safely on the road, she broke her silence. "What the hell was that?! Goddamn Hobgoblin!" she swore to Wilson as she ripped the Panama hat from her head. "I can have the dress laundered, but this hat is completely ruined!"

# Epilogue

Mount Vernon Place, Maryland, USA
15th of May, 3:52 p.m. (GMT-4)

It didn't take long for ladies' tea to go from an intimate gathering to a legitimate party. By the time Aunt Bethany produced a list of names, there wasn't a venue that could accommodate that large of a group on such short notice, especially during the weekend of Preakness Stakes. Fortunately, the Moncrief family home was spacious with a well-kept lawn and lovely views.

It had been a while since Moncrief hosted a party of her own. While she'd kept up with esoteric duties, estate maintenance, shareholders meetings, and charitable organizations, entertaining had progressively fallen to the wayside since she'd joined the Salt Mine. It wasn't practical when she could be called away at the drop of a hat.

There was a time when she relished planning the perfect party; centerpieces, flower arrangements, the selection of canapés and hors d'oeuvres, seating, entertainment—the details were endless. Now, it all seemed rather trivial, the kind of thing people focused on when they were avoiding all that was bigger than them.

When planning got tedious, she reminded herself that this was for Aunt Bethany, who was an actual blood relation and not an honorary aunt. Her mother's older sister was the designated cool aunt, the one Moncrief would go to when she was in a jam and didn't want her parents to know. The one she went to for real answers and advice, not the sugarcoated ones adults were supposed to tell children. The one that played devil's advocate when her parents worried that she wasn't on the right track. Their relatively recent disagreement on marriage and children notwithstanding, Aunt Bethany was a good egg.

It had all come together at the eleventh hour; even the weather cooperated. Moncrief had not lost her touch, even if her girlish enthusiasm for such things had waned. Like every hostess, all she could see were the deficits, but her mind was put to ease when the guests arrived and marveled at the picture-perfect garden party.

As she circulated among her guests in one of her favorite tea dresses—an Unger off-the-shoulder fit-and-flare with small white flowers on Kelly green—she had to admit it was nice to see the grounds full of people enjoying a summer's day before the races. Carmarthen was no stranger to hospitality. When she was a child, her parents often had company and she had heard tales of the galas and epic parties held in simpler times.

As the afternoon wore on, the crowd thinned as people left for previous engagements. Tomorrow was Preakness Stakes, the second jewel in the Triple Crown, and all the metro area was gripped in celebration. Tonight's fireworks in the Inner Harbor were the finale to a week of public events, and there would be a slew of parties in Charm City's homes, bars, restaurants, private clubs, and yachts. Baltimore refused to be outdone by Louisville.

When the festivities had adequately died down, Moncrief slipped inside and retired her warm smile and affected cheer. She was on her home turf and ironically, she had fewer social engagements this weekend than she did attending the Derby. The only thing she couldn't say no to had just ended.

When she entered the foyer, she heard someone playing the piano in the music room. She had taken lessons in her youth and kept the shiny Yamaha concert grand tuned out of sentimentality but rarely played these days. Drawn to the melody, she opened the door wide and found her aunt working away at the keys. As she swayed with the music, the diaphanous layers of her shift dress drifted with her.

Her pensive brown eyes looked up at the door but her fingers never left the piano. "Hey sweetie," she greeted Moncrief. "Is the party over?"

"Just about. Gerard will take care of the stragglers," she replied as she approached. When called upon, her faithful butler had the strategy, cunning, and iron hand of a field general. She had nothing to worry about with him in charge of clean up. She planted a kiss on Bethany's upturned cheek and took a seat near her. "Did you have fun?"

"It was wonderful," she said as she glided her hands over the ivory. "It almost makes up for ditching me before and after the Derby."

"I didn't ditch you," Moncrief protested. "Other time sensitive things required my attention. I wouldn't dream of ditching my favorite aunt," she added sweetly and batted her big blue eyes in exaggeration.

Bethany rolled her eyes. "You are just like your mother." Her statement elicited an honest smile from her niece. "That wasn't a compliment. She and your father would take off at the drop of a dime with flimsy excuses, too."

Moncrief was about to object, but the older woman abruptly stopped playing and held up one hand before she could speak. "I don't know what you are doing and I don't want to know. Just promise me you'll be careful."

*That's why you're the cool aunt*, Moncrief thought as she sidled up on the bench and gave her aunt a hug from the side. "I promise."

Bethany took her at her word and resumed her sonata a few bars from where she'd left off. "I saw you talking to a very handsome young man at the party, the tall slim one with the spiky brown hair and pretty blue eyes," she commented innocently.

"Ugh. Justin Peterson. He invited himself and I let him stay as decoration. Tech new money and not a practitioner," she bluntly filled in her aunt.

The older woman sighed. "That's too bad." She could overlook the fact that he wasn't an old family, but it seemed a waste for her niece to marry a non-practitioner. "But there are other fish in the sea."

"I appreciate your concern for my love life, but I'm fine, Aunt Bethany," Moncrief insisted. "I have a lot on my plate and I'm not in a rush to tie myself down."

The pianist shrugged nonchalantly. "I get it. You're happy with the way things are, but it may not always be enough."

"Give up a life I find satisfying to get married and have a family for the future ennui I might feel if I didn't," Moncrief restated what she'd heard. "You know how silly that sounds, right?"

"Alicia Elspeth Hovdenak Moncrief, I said no such thing!" her aunt corrected her. The sound of her full name put Moncrief's entire being on alert and for a brief moment, she felt like a child that had been caught doing something naughty. "I'm proud of the work you've done to keep your parent's legacy going and I'm sure they would be proud too. I'm just saying you don't have to do it alone. Even your mother had your father."

"I've got help," Moncrief objected.

"You have staff, social acquaintances, and professional contacts," she countered. "I'm talking about someone who is always in your corner and has your back come hell or high water."

Moncrief bit her lip. She couldn't tell her aunt about the Salt Mine, but she wanted to smooth things over and fell back on her charms. "Why do I need a husband for that when I have you?"

Bethany shook her head. "Just like Anna," she muttered.

"I'm not categorically opposed to getting married," Moncrief informed her in all seriousness. "I just haven't found someone suitable that can keep up with me."

The pianist let out a short laugh. "Good luck with that, sweetie. Pretty much all men have to be massaged into spouse material."

"You're not helping your case," Moncrief said drily.

"Do you honestly think your father could keep up with your mother when they met?" her aunt asked gently. "He knew he wanted to be with her and picked up the pace. And she was worried she was never going to find someone who really understood her. But they found each other, and I have to believe there's someone out there for you too. Someone who will help you bloom, not stifle you."

It was hard for Moncrief to imagine her parents as they would have been at her age. The stories had all been sanitized and the hardships expunged by the time they reached her ears, and her mother died before Moncrief had reached the age where women felt like they could tell their daughters the truth about such things. Aunt Bethany's hints were the closest Moncrief had to seeing her parents as real people.

Bethany finished the sonata with a reverent pause before swiveling around to address her niece directly. "I know it's hard to meet people and find a genuine connection given your position," she said sympathetically. "Why do you think I've been throwing men your way?"

"Because you desperately want to spoil my children?" Moncrief joked.

"Because I don't want you to wake up one day wanting more, only to discover it's too late. Everyone your age thinks they have time, but it goes by faster than you think."

"I'll take it under advisement," Moncrief eventually conceded. "Thankfully, I still have you looking out for me."

Bethany curtly nodded her head when she saw her niece was really listening. "Damn straight."

## THE END

The agents of The Salt Mine will return in *Fair Game*

Printed in Great Britain
by Amazon

81156143R00129